# Married to a Dead Man

*An Aimee Talcos Mystery*

by

## Elizabeth Lanham

For information, email **Cozy Cat Press**, cozycatpress@aol.com  or visit our website at: www.cozycatpress.com

COZY CAT
P R E S S

ISBN:  978-1-946063-27-4

Printed in the United States of America

Cover design by Paula Ellenberger
www.paulaellenberger.com

1 2 3 4 5 6 7 8 9 10

To Mom and Dad, I love you

# Chapter 1

"Do I know you?"

A deep, raspy voice broke into my consciousness as I reached out to turn the next page of my novel. A shadow fell across the small black print, effectively blocking the sunlight that streamed around me. I swallowed, thinking in the back of my mind that I recognized the voice coming from above, yet at the same time knowing it wasn't my husband.

I looked up, making eye contact with an elderly gentleman, unknown and yet familiar. My eyes narrowed as he stepped toward me with a somewhat amused expression.

"Should I know you?" he asked.

I placed my index finger inside the pages and closed my book. Extending my right hand, I attempted a confident smile and tried to hide my nervousness while greeting him.

"I don't believe we've met," I began, trying to pull my hand back from a rather firm grip.

"Alfred Talcos." His smile grew, this time into a toothy and surprisingly charming grin.

As he finally let go of my hand, he clarified, "This is my house."

I abruptly stood up from the deck chair where I had escaped, stumbling backwards before awkwardly regaining my balance.

Standing before me was a grey-haired gentleman, barely taller than myself, with a slight stoop. His whiskers needed trimming and his wrinkled suit and loosened tie lent him a travel-worn appearance. His eyes were eerily similar to my husband's and were patiently watching me, waiting for me to introduce myself.

I wasn't quite sure what to say. I knew who he was, maybe not by sight but definitely by name. So how do you tell the owner of the house you have just crashed, and also the only remaining relative of the man you had impulsively married, that he was now your grandfather-in-law?

I settled for the easy way out.

"I'm Aimee," I identified myself. "I'm here with Declan."

Then, like a coward, I averted my eyes from his to gaze out at the rolling waves, blue sky and sweeping clouds resting calmly on the horizon.

My hand came up to rub the back of my neck. Declan and I had arrived at his grandfather's beach house just yesterday. Our three-day-old marriage was unusual to say the least and I wasn't sure how to explain it.

There was a silence and I could sense that Mr. Talcos was waiting for me to go on. I stubbornly kept my face turned toward the ocean. In the distance two sailboats appeared to be on a collision course as the morning sun bore down on them, a plausible analogy for Declan's and my strange relationship.

I glanced back at Mr. Talcos and smiled shakily, giving him the opportunity to speak first. He finally cleared his throat and gave a slight nod.

"You are a friend of my grandson," he said, as if explaining it to himself. I nodded and bit my lower lip. I was, in a manner of speaking, a sort of friend.

"What brings you two here?"

"We arrived yesterday," I explained, hoping to make a decent attempt at sounding like everything was normal. "Declan was hoping to find you at home and thought if we waited a day or so, you would turn up."

That was mostly true. Only he had kind of hoped his grandfather would stay away until after we were gone, preferably without him ever knowing we had been here.

To be honest, I still didn't entirely understand why we had come to his grandfather's house in the first place; not that Declan consulted me when he made any of his plans. Several times over the past two weeks a question or two had sat on the tip of my tongue, dying to be asked. Instead, every time I got up the nerve, something deep inside would shut me down and I would end up shelving my concerns for another day.

Pulling myself together, I turned toward the house, gesturing toward the sliding door with my hand.

"I believe we'll find Declan in the study. Why don't we go look for him?" I grabbed my bag with the book, checked to make sure my cell was inside, and then slung it over my shoulder.

Leading the way through the sliding glass doors, I sensed rather than saw Mr. Talcos following me. Taking a deep breath to calm my racing heart, I thought to myself, *You'd better be in the study, Declan Talcos. Things just got that much more complicated.*

I grabbed my phone out and put it in my back pocket. Then I dropped my sack on the kitchen counter, making as much noise as possible. I walked down the hall toward the study, calling out for Declan, hoping to give him a head's up that we had company.

We entered the book-lined room together—Mr. Talcos and I—his toes almost stepping on my heels. The room was dark and the drapes were closed with only a splash of sunlight coming between them.

I noted the laptop sitting open on the desk but with no sign of Declan. I walked around to look at the screen and noticed the screensaver had turned on.

I frowned. Maybe he'd gone upstairs.

Pulling out my cell phone, I glanced up at Declan's grandfather who was standing on the other side of the desk, watching me.

"I'll just text him you're here," I said, trying to sound friendly and not frantic. Surely Declan wouldn't just leave me here with his grandfather?

Mr. Talcos nodded and I noticed his amiable smile was no longer present. He sauntered around to the window and drew the curtains while I tapped out a message. As the brilliant light penetrated the room my eyes adjusted and focused on the floor beneath me. What I saw caused my heart to stop and for a second I couldn't breath. Unable to look away, I gripped my cell phone tightly and let out an ear-splitting scream.

## Chapter 2

Declan's unseeing eyes stared up at me from beneath the desk, his body stuffed in an unnatural position with only the head sticking out. It was ghastly but made even more so because his face was upside down, his frown now a smile. Dark blood trickled down his forehead from the large bullet wound in its center and pooled on the carpet.

Disbelieving tremors shook me and I continued to scream.

I sensed Mr. Talcos approaching and I looked up, fear instantly putting me on guard. He stepped toward me cautiously, as if unsure of my mental condition, and looked like he was debating whether to look under the desk or run out of the room. I backed away, the body of my husband before me as I bumped into the window.

Some basic instinct within told me that I was safe as I saw Mr. Talcos coming around the end of the desk. If he had anything to do with Declan lying there, surly he would not be looking at me like I was a crazy person. My screams turned into a whimper and I began to cry, shutting my eyes for the first time.

Instantly I opened them again. There was no relief. Declan's ghastly face stayed before me, already imprinted on my mind.

My grandfather-in-law took one look under the table and his face turned ashen. He retreated toward the door without looking away from the desk and then commanded me in a curt tone to call the police. I stared at him.

At this moment I was faced with a terrible dilemma. Declan was currently hiding from the law. I was abetting him. Either I could call the police and risk putting myself in their custody or I could ignore the command and try to get as far away as possible. To my knowledge, no one was aware I existed except Declan's grandfather and he only knew me as his grandson's friend, Aimee. Could I possibly escape now that Mr. Talcos had seen me?

Another thought intruded. No one knew Declan's recent whereabouts, except me and whoever had murdered him. Would I be implicated for more than Declan's crime if I were found with him dead? Would they blame me for it?

"Aimee."

Mr. Talcos broke my reverie.

"Declan was shot. You are holding your phone. Call the police."

As Declan's open but unseeing eyes stared up at me, I quickly put thoughts of my own well-being aside and dialed 911. The call was short and to the point. Surprisingly I was able to give information to the operator without breaking down.

After I hung up, I walked toward Mr. Talcos who stood watching me from the doorway.

"They want us to wait outside the room and not touch anything. They'll be here in the next ten minutes."

I wondered at the calmness in my voice as I made my way out of the room, stepping past Mr. Talcos. As he closed the door behind me, I hiccupped and felt tears blur my eyes once again. Sitting down in the hall I began to sob until I could barely breathe. A brown paper bag was pushed in front of me and the ragged voice of Mr. Talcos spoke, telling me to breathe into it.

That is how the police and EMTs found us only minutes later: me breathing into a bag and Mr. Talcos stooped over, telling me to slow down my breath.

We were ushered into the living room to wait while the police made their initial inspection. The furniture was white and matched the eyelet curtains. There was a beach feel with images of seashells decorating the walls and adorning the lamps. As the minutes ticked by and my breathing remained controlled, I distractedly wondered who had decorated it.

Without forethought, I commented to Mr. Talcos about the lovely interior and then fell silent in embarrassment. His grandson had just been shot in the head and I wanted to talk about the color scheme of his living room? What was wrong with me? Thankfully Mr. Talcos acknowledged my remark with a polite nod and then let silence refill the room.

It felt like hours passed but was probably less than a half hour before a tall young man in a white polo shirt and grey khakis came into the room. He identified himself as Adam Harrison, the detective assigned to investigate Declan's case.

Unfortunately he had more than a few questions, none of which I was eager to answer.

"How did you know the deceased?" he began after taking our names and writing them in a small notebook he held against his knee.

I gave him my maiden name and then shrank back in the chair in an effort to avoid attention. Fortunately it was like being in school. As long as I didn't make eye contact, I felt like I couldn't be called on. I listened as Mr. Talcos explained his presence and in the meantime tried to come up with a plan for what to say when my turn came.

How to reply? My relationship with Declan was complicated to say the least and I don't think I could have described it without saying too much. If I explained how we met, I'd soon be telling the detective everything.

Was it better to say as little as possible? Would the detective even want to know about the wedding? I assumed our marriage was legal and binding, even if it was only of three days duration and had been performed on the spur of the moment for two people who had lied about their birth cities, current residence and job titles.

The same feeling of self-preservation that had led me to think I should hightail it out of the study earlier reared its ugly head and the panicky feeling had me looking around again for the paper bag. Then there was my conscience whispering, albeit very softly, that Declan had been running from the law, trying to prove his own innocence, and was now dead. Didn't I owe it to him to finish what he started and help find his murderer?

I glanced at Mr. Talcos who was explaining that this was his house and that Declan was his grandson. I watched his face as he spoke. He was barely holding himself together, his countenance grey and grief-stricken. He paused, taking a moment to regain his composure, before going on with his story.

His tale was simple. He had driven to the house in a taxi from the airport after flying into Boston that morning from New York. He had discovered me on the back deck almost immediately and then the two of us had found Declan. No, he didn't know who I was. I had introduced myself as Declan's friend. He had been too shocked to find Declan dead to wonder who I was. He hadn't been able to think about anything else after that.

In that moment I was certain of one thing. I didn't want to say anything that might cause Mr. Talcos more grief.

When it was my turn, I asked to speak to the detective privately and Declan's grandfather didn't object. Detective Harrison politely asked him to wait upstairs in his room.

My eyes trailed him as he slowly pushed up from the chair and walked out. I wondered vaguely which room was his. I was pretty sure Declan and I had been using two of the guestrooms, at least I hoped I hadn't been sleeping in his grandfather's room.

I was turning to face the detective when he asked without preamble, "Mrs. Talcos, can you explain why there are BOLOs out for your husband in over seven states, why he has been missing for over three weeks after being accused of embezzlement, and why he is dead?"

I felt like the wind had been knocked out of me and for a moment I couldn't breathe. Apparently the police knew more about me than I realized and telling them about my marriage wasn't going to require any courage on my part.

Once again a paper bag was held out to me and a steady voice told me to slow my breathing. Detective Harrison remained at my side as once again I hyperventilated.

After I regained control, I leaned back and looked at the serious and slightly suspicious man squatting beside me. His face was handsome although his nose was a little long. His dark hair complimented his blue eyes and fair skin, making the five o'clock shadow on his jaw stand out.

His closeness, and the fact he knew Declan was my husband caused me to jerk back. For a moment I thought about lying, denying knowledge of everything he had just told me, and even claiming insanity, because if I had ever felt crazy and out of control, it was now.

"Are you feeling calmer?" he asked as he stood and stepped away. "I'd like to continue our interview."

A muscle jumped in his cheek and I realized that I was starting to get on his nerves. I sniffed and then blurted out the question foremost in my mind, "How did you know Declan was my husband?"

His eyes narrowed suspiciously and I felt my breathing accelerate. I picked up the bag and began blowing into it without any prompting.

"Your name and picture were released last night as a person of interest in Declan's case."

"By who?" My voice was muffled as I spoke into the bag.

His voice was stern as he spoke over my huffing, "The FBI. Did you think you could get married by a government entity and not have it discovered?"

I hadn't thought anything about it. I was just helping Declan.

"But you didn't say anything when you first saw me?" I put the bag down, trying to wrap my mind around the fact that he knew who I was and glad now that I hadn't made a run for it.

He pursed his lips and I could tell he was no longer trying to hide his irritation.

"I think I'll ask the questions. The FBI is investigating Declan for his part in the embezzlement of Autem Viris but I'm investigating his murder, and preferably in an orderly manner. I need you to cooperate."

He paused to let that sink in and then began again, "How did you know the deceased?"

## Chapter 3

I took a deep breath. There was no good reason to withhold information now. Declan was dead. Nothing I said was going to make me look less guilty. I had disappeared with a man wanted for embezzlement and then two weeks later been found in another state with him shot in the head. I couldn't make my situation any worse.

I began my narrative slowly, hoping and praying that I was somewhat coherent. The events of the past few weeks were confusing, even to me, and I had lived through them.

"I met Declan in Memphis. I was working a part-time job in a stadium, cleaning stands and restrooms before and after games and shows."

My voice sounded pathetically weak and I cleared my throat, erasing the scratchiness, "I was in the ladies' room mopping the floor when he broke in, looking scared and exhausted. He told me the police were coming after him for something he hadn't done and that he needed more time to prove his innocence."

I swallowed, buying time for myself and trying not to remember the way Declan's eyes had bored into mine the day he'd walked into my life, making me feel like I was his only hope. The moment of doubt as I stood there, wondering if I should or should not help him. His pleading expression searing into me while I leaned into the mop, aware that I didn't know anything about him. Then I realized not only was I not afraid but I felt a strange and uncanny desire to trust him. I wanted to do whatever I could, if only to erase the look of desperation from his face. A split second decision, but even as I faced the detective, I didn't regret it.

I lifted my chin and looked directly at the man, "I locked him in the cabinet beneath the sink where the cleaning supplies were kept. Police officers and security from the stadium came in and made a thorough check of the stalls, but they never thought to have me open the cabinets. After they left, I helped Declan escape through a side door to the parking lot and then hid him in the trunk of my car. After we were a couple miles away, I stopped and let him out. He wanted me to leave him on the side of the road, but I offered to drive him to Georgia. He climbed back into the trunk and stayed there until we were across the border when I let him out again."

"I'm surprised you weren't picked up on the stadium cameras," the detective said, his pen stopping as he looked up at me.

I hadn't thought of that. Declan had. "It was dark. He used my coat and scarf as a disguise. And I was parked in employee parking, not very well-lit."

Detective Harrison looked down and made another note before asking, "Were you forced to drive him?"

I shook my head, stressing what I'd already said. "No, I offered to drive him. After we got to Georgia, he tried to go off on his own, but I said I was willing to go as far as he needed."

What had started out as a two-hour drive quickly turned into a two-week, life-changing adventure.

"At first I only intended to bring him across state lines but that's not what happened. We kept going. We drove on back roads, avoiding major highways, and finally ended up in Little Rock."

The detective seemed to hound me on my involvement. "And through it all you were a willing participant?"

"I went voluntarily."

I felt my cheeks grow warm as he eye-balled me, weighing my answers with whatever thoughts he was entertaining.

"Then you got married," continued Adam, his eyebrows raised, "to someone you'd just met and who told you he was wanted by the law?"

I nodded and choked, putting the bag to my mouth again.

I had always known that there was no love in our relationship, at least not on Declan's side. Affection, maybe, but nothing like when a man cherishes a woman. Our marriage was one of convenience and, even with more time, I don't think he could have learned to love me. Maybe it was our age difference. Maybe it was our situation. Maybe it was because Declan had too many secrets. Or maybe it was me.

As I breathed into the brown paper, my mind drifted back to the night before we were married.

Declan had turned to face me in the car after I filled up the tank at a tiny one-hose gas station. I had just buckled myself into the passenger seat when he said, "Aimee, I know this is sudden, but I think we need to get married. This way I can go underground and as my wife you can continue to manage my accounts and protect my interests."

He'd paused and then continued, as if trying to convince both of us, "You'll be well provided for and this way I'll stay connected here. No one can get information out of you as my wife and after I get this mess straightened out, I'll come back. We'll get divorced, split things fifty-fifty, which will make you comfortable for the rest of your life. I'm thinking it'll take maybe a year tops."

I'd remained silent, taking in his offer.

"I won't take more than a year of your life from you."

His eyes had connected with mine, the gas station light illuminating half his face. He'd smiled tentatively, hopefully, "I trust you. You trust me, don't you? Seriously, Aimee, I don't have anyone else I can ask for help."

I had naively said yes, but I remembered being hesitant and worried. If Declan was innocent, why was he leaving?

By that point, I knew in my heart that even though I was uncertain whether or not he was completely innocent, I would do whatever he needed me to do. If marrying helped him, I would marry him.

Detective Harrison cleared his throat and I realized the bag was now in my lap, clenched tightly in my fist. I slowly loosened my grip.

"You were married," he said, drawing me back to the present.

I swallowed and choked out, "We spent a few days in Little Rock and on the last day we were married at the city courthouse."

I remembered but didn't tell him how nervous Declan was that day. Not about getting married, but about being discovered. I don't think he took a full breath until we were a good twelve hours away.

"Then what happened?"

"The next day we climbed into the car and drove directly here, stopping only for food, gas, and to spend the night somewhere. We arrived thinking Mr. Talcos would be absent. Declan planned to get his boat and head up to Canada if he couldn't figure things out here. I assumed he meant if he couldn't find a way to prove his innocence, but I never really knew exactly what he was looking for."

I left out the part about him telling me this morning that it would be a while before he could prove anything and that he was planning to disappear, regardless of what he had or hadn't found, the day he was murdered.

The detective's eyes narrowed, "Where were you going to stay after he left?"

I gestured around me vaguely. "Here, I guess. I don't really know."

"Did you murder him?"

My mouth dropped open.

"Of course not!"

"Do you know who did?"

"Absolutely not! Declan was alive when I saw him last. We had breakfast together and then he went into the study to work on the computer. I took my book out to the porch. I didn't go inside or see anyone until Mr. Talcos showed up and we found him together."

The eyebrows went up again.

"So you're telling me that you met this guy two weeks ago, impulsively gave up your job, basically everything you had, to go with him who knows where. Then you married him, just happened to find him murdered and…" his voice lowered as he enunciated the last words slowly, "you have no idea what happened?"

I flinched at the accusation in his voice but nodded just the same. In a sense I agreed, how could I not be involved? As described by Detective Harrison, I was either a murderess or insane.

"Detective," I began.

"Adam," he cut me off.

"Adam," I started again, vaguely wondering why he cared what I called him, "I realize this whole story sounds crazy. I knew from the get-go that Declan was hiding from the law and that in abetting him, I was now guilty of breaking the law." I paused, thinking how condemning that sounded.

I tried again, "But I want to make one thing clear. Until yesterday, I never knew why we were hiding from the law. Declan turned the news on last night and that was the first time I saw or heard anything regarding the embezzlement."

"You never asked him what he'd done?" Adam's expression was skeptical.

I paused, remembering the conversation Declan and I had shared our first day together. After we'd crossed the Georgia border and I'd offered to keep driving as far as he needed, I found myself filled with trepidation. What was I doing? I didn't know anything more about this man than that he claimed he was fleeing capture for a crime he hadn't committed. Oh, and he had a face I trusted.

Sensing my fear, Declan gently reached out from the passenger seat where he now sat and covered my hand on the steering wheel. I looked into his green, earnest eyes, searching for something, possibly reassurance.

"You don't have to do this," he said, with sincerity, "I can get by from here."

He had wanted me to decide. How young and foolish I must have seemed to him. How desperate he must have been. It occurred to me now how easy it would have been for him to hit me over the head, take my car and drive away. He could have been lying to me from the get-go, yet I had believed every word.

I had turned back to face the highway unfolding in front of us and realized I was no longer afraid. His insistence that I not help him did more to cement my determination than any begging or force would have.

"Just tell me one thing," I'd said, not wanting to ask but feeling a burning desire to know, "Did you kill anyone?"

Declan had released his breath and I looked over as he barked out a short laugh. "No, I absolutely did not."

His grip tightened on my hand before he pulled back and adjusted his seatbelt.

"Come on. Let's get off this highway."

I didn't say anything as I turned on the engine and shifted into drive. I had believed him when he'd told me he was innocent at the stadium and so I believed him when he said he hadn't killed anyone. Anticipation of something new and exciting crept over me and I glanced at him one more time before merging onto the main road. Really, what did I have to lose?

Now as I faced my interrogator, my reasoning seemed flimsy and naive. Rather than explain the instant bond that I had felt with Declan, I answered the detective's original question painfully and like I was on a witness stand.

"Did I ask what he had done? Not really. I never wanted details. I believed him when he said he was innocent. And when I learned that he was wanted for embezzlement, I believed him when he said it wasn't true."

## Chapter 4

Eventually the detective, or Adam as he now wanted to be called, moved on with his line of questioning. When we got around to the actual discovery of the body, he asked point by point where I'd been and what I'd been doing up to the moment I found Declan. He wanted to know who was aware we were coming to Maine. He wanted to know the name of every single person we'd seen in the last three days or anyone that Declan might have contacted.

These questions were senseless to me. As far as I knew, no one knew of our whereabouts and the sum total of people we'd encountered since arriving in Maine was zero.

"One more question," Adam said after I explained how Mr. Talcos and I had waited in the hall for the police. Thinking we were done, I had moved to the edge of my chair in anticipation of being dismissed. I settled back against my seat and waited, certain the exhaustion showed on my face.

He contemplated me for a moment, framing his chin with his index fingers and tapping them slowly against his whiskered cheeks, "I know you believed Declan was innocent before today. In light of what has happened, do you still think that?"

I bit my bottom lip, unsure how to respond. After finding Declan murdered, I had no idea what to think. Everything was in confusion and if I thought too hard about it, I was pretty sure I would be hyperventilating again.

Adam's poker face watched as these thoughts flickered through my mind. I didn't have an answer for him.

"Was anyone else involved in your escape? Or do you know of anyone who would want to hurt your husband?"

My immediate response was to shake my head with conviction but instead I stopped and considered. I hadn't known Declan very well and to say I was privy to his plans was an understatement. He rarely told me what he was thinking and even more rarely was I able to guess. I knew he was afraid. I knew he was running. I had been told it was from the law for a crime he hadn't committed, but what if there was more to the story? What if he hadn't told me the whole truth? What if he was also running from somebody?

I looked up at Adam, who was impatiently waiting for me to answer. Slowly I shook my head in the negative, offering a pretty pathetic answer for all the time I took to think of it.

"I can't think of anyone and he certainly never mentioned being afraid of anything, except maybe of getting caught."

Adam looked like he wasn't sure he believed me.

"And you never suspected he might have a partner or someone he was in contact with?"

His question made me think of the one time I had actually witnessed Declan talking to anyone besides myself or the occasional gas station attendant.

About to share something that was probably completely unrelated to his murder, I said nervously, "Once, before we were married, Declan woke me in the middle of the night and told me we had to leave. I think we were in Georgia at the time. We left the room key on the bedside table, climbed into my car and took off. It must have been a little before midnight."

Declan woke me out of a deep sleep by shaking my arm and calling my name softly. My initial groggy response was followed by a moment of panic as I realized he was touching me. That feeling had quickly fled as it penetrated my consciousness that he was telling me we had to go.

Vague, sleep-drunk memories arose in my mind as I remembered grabbing my bag and following him to the car with bleary, half-closed eyes.

"I was nearly asleep sitting in the passenger seat but I remember looking outside for Declan who was taking longer than I expected to get in the car. He was standing by the door, his phone held up to his ear. He hung up before climbing in the car. It was unusual but I said nothing. Then Declan drove while I slept."

Adam made a mark in his notebook, "Do you remember what hotel you were staying in?"

I rattled off the name of the hotel, certain that this information was less than useful. Adam dutifully recorded it and then closed his notebook. Our interview was over.

He left me sitting alone, trying to take in what had just happened. He hadn't mentioned pressing charges or putting me under arrest for murder or embezzlement.

For a moment I scarcely breathed. Then I exhaled and bent over my knees, hugging my stomach with both arms and trying to stop the fear from twisting my insides. I had no idea what would happen next.

I stayed like that until Declan's grandfather re-entered the room. He came in silently except for a slight wheeze and took the chair opposite me. I sat up to look at him and noticed his face was haggard and drawn. I felt the stirrings of pity in my heart.

Shifting to the edge of my chair, I leaned forward and offered to find him something to drink. He declined and I began to feel uncomfortable as he stared unblinkingly at me.

"I think I would like to know a little more about you," he began, his gaze wavering, "Who are you really? And why are you here?"

I bit my lip in what was becoming a nervous habit and wondered where to begin and how much to say.

Declan hadn't told me much about his grandfather. Once, when we arrived at the beautiful, waterfront house and I had remarked on how big it was, he had mentioned that his grandfather was wealthy but aside from this I had known little more than that he existed.

Ironically, I had learned last night on the news that Mr. Talcos was Declan's only remaining relative. I had also learned that he was a part of Declan's company, though in what way they hadn't explained.

The look on Mr. Talcos' face changed while I wrestled with my thoughts and suddenly I saw that he himself was struggling with grief and pain. Something inside me gave way and I began to tell him everything, everything I knew anyway, and all that had happened to me since I'd met his grandson.

Throughout my narrative, the elderly gentleman sitting across from me remained silently absorbed in my story. From meeting Declan to marrying Declan to finding out the night before that he was wanted by the FBI, I held nothing back.

I told him things I hadn't told Adam. Like how much I trusted Declan and how much I wanted to help him. Instead of answering questions like I was being cross-examined, I became so emotional that by the end I was crying and at the same time practically shouting that we would find Declan's murderer, no matter what.

As I sniffed, regaining control of myself after this rather brash statement, Mr. Talcos leaned back in his chair, eyes on me, his gaze unreadable. I crossed my legs and looked down at my lap, shaking hands gripping each other tightly.

His voice softened and he murmured compassionately, "You poor child."

Standing up, he made his way over to where I sat and gently reached down for my hand. Feeling awkward with him towering above me, I rose to stand beside him, my hand still gripped by his.

He was barely an inch taller than me, so we were practically at eye level as he said, "I am so sorry Declan dragged you into all of this. He shouldn't have."

He paused and for the first time I wondered how much he knew about Declan.

His voice was gruff as he continued, "I want you to know that come what may, you have my support. And if you need anything, you only need ask."

Then he let me go and stepped back. He returned to his chair and eased back into it.

"Go on up to your room and take a rest," he said, "I need to think."

Feeling slightly dazed, I did as he commanded, slipping up the stairs and ignoring the voices I could hear coming from the study. Closing my door to blessed silence, I crawled into bed and fell into a dreamless sleep.

## Chapter 5

By the time I awoke it was past four in the afternoon. I stretched and lifted my head, feeling some puffiness around my eyes and a slight headache weighing me down.

It was a moment before I remembered the events of the day and then they came back with a vengeance. Slowly pulling myself from bed, I made my way to the small bathroom adjoining my bedroom. I took a long shower, hoping the warm water would clear my mind and maybe even wash away memories of Declan's face with a bullet in it.

Unfortunately, that was a futile endeavor.

As I dressed, I thought about Declan, dead under the desk. Someone had shot him and must have used a silencer, as I'd heard nothing. Of course, the sound of the ocean was loud out on the back deck, but certainly I would have heard a gunshot.

Whoever had shot him had also been strong enough to stuff his body beneath the desk. Neither Mr. Talcos nor I seemed physically capable of that. Declan had been a tall, well-built man and I didn't think I could move him. His grandfather looked even weaker than I.

As I slowly descended the stairs, the house appeared deserted. I made my way down the hall, noting the fading light. Hearing voices, I approached the study and found yellow caution tape strung across the doorway and two detectives inside, one of them Adam.

He looked up as I stopped in front of the plastic strip, careful to remain outside the room. A brief smile was directed at me before he murmured something to the other detective, an older man with greying hair, and came towards me.

"Were you able to sleep?" he asked, his manner solicitous and yet impersonal.

I nodded, turning away from him to look about the room. I noted the desk had been moved and Declan's body no longer reposed beneath.

"Have you found anything?" I asked, my voice squeaky and breathier than I would have liked. Seeing the room again was bringing back the image of Declan's open, unseeing eyes and his lifeless body. I slowed my breathing.

Adam turned and surveyed the room, before saying, "It appears the safe on the wall was disturbed."

I looked across, surprised to see a picture knocked awry and a door hanging open from a metal box set inside the wall. I must have missed it my first time in the room. With the half-light from the closed drapes obscuring my vision and the subsequent discovery of Declan's body, this was of course understandable.

"At this point, we really don't know much. We're looking into the possibility of Declan interrupting a robbery. We searched the house and premises and have yet to find a murder weapon."

"I highly doubt that this was a random break-in," I said without thinking. "Not after everything else Declan went through."

"Is there more you'd like to tell me about that?" he asked, quick to jump on my last statement.

I shrank back, realizing I'd set myself up. Mutely, I shook my head.

Frowning, he waited for me to change my mind before going on, "Okay. Well, we're examining all the possibilities. If you have anything that would help shed light on this, it would be much appreciated."

I had nothing to say in response to this, so I looked back at the older man across the room. He was closing up the drawers on the desk. It looked like the computer had already been removed.

Adam and I stood for a while watching the other detective at work. Then Adam cleared his throat and began, "My men tell me that two guest rooms upstairs are occupied. You said in your statement that no one else was here except for you and your husband."

I reddened and looked away, unsure what he would think about Declan's and my unusual relationship. For the first time I understood the natural assumption that a couple was intimate, regardless of the reason they married.

I hurried to explain, "Declan and I had separate rooms. Although we were married, it was more like a business contract. We weren't involved."

"Well, maybe not physically," Adam said intuitively, causing my blush to deepen. I knew he referred to my emotional involvement; after all I had left everything to follow this man to the ends of the earth, or in this case: Maine.

My eyes became teary as I looked down. I wiped them and then glanced over, surprised to see a look of empathy cross his face before the cop mask fell back into place.

"So I'm guessing you don't know what was in the safe?" Adam asked, changing the subject and kindly allowing me to act as if his rather personal observation hadn't discomfited me.

I made an effort to regain my composure before answering, "No, I didn't even know there was a safe."

The question that had been pressing upon me from the moment I'd first called 911 rose to the surface, and I blurted out, "Am I going to be arrested?"

Adam pivoted toward me once more and eyed me speculatively, "Not tonight."

He paused as if gauging my reaction. I'm sure the relief was written across my face.

"We may have evidence to show you weren't in the house during the murder. You are, however, a person of interest and the FBI will want to interview you. Until this investigation is concluded and we release you, you will stay here."

I was so relieved that I was off the hook for the night, that it completely went over my head that Adam said they might have evidence I wasn't the murderer. I didn't even think to ask what that evidence was. I was too busy thinking about not spending the night in jail. Anything would be better than that. At least, I assumed it would be better. I hadn't spent a night in jail before.

After our brief exchange, I headed to the kitchen where I searched the cabinets for something to make for dinner. I wasn't hungry and eating was the last thing I wanted to do, but the process of cooking appealed to me. It would keep my hands busy and my mind distracted, hopefully. Besides, maybe Mr. Talcos would be hungry. At the very least, he should eat something.

I set about putting together a simple repast of omelets, toast and home fries. As I chopped up the onions and potatoes, I thought about the safe. If anyone could tell me what had been inside, it was Declan's grandfather. He could probably also tell me why the FBI suspected Declan of the embezzlement. For the first time I realized I had a lot of unanswered questions about my deceased husband's alleged crime.

As I put plates covered with food into the oven to keep warm, I considered my options. Was it foolish to ask questions? Did I really want to know more? Maybe it was best to just let the FBI and police do their job.

The last thing I wanted was to draw more attention to myself.

Undecided, I went in search of Mr. Talcos. I found him on the back deck, gazing at the ocean. His shoulders were sagging and his entire demeanor struck me as one defeated.

I walked up and stood beside him. For a few minutes we watched the waves pound the shore, one after another, each one hitting at a slightly different place on the sand. It was dusk, the waves a murky grey-green as clouds obscured the rapidly disappearing sun.

*Sort of like life*, I thought, putting my hands on the railing and staring at the rolling surf. *It just keeps coming. You can't stop it from happening and sometimes it takes you down.* I frowned. *Hmmm and then you can't get up again before the next wave hits.*

My mind drifted back to the years before I'd met Declan. Before he had pulled me out of that stadium restroom and turned my life upside down. I was the youngest of three, my two older siblings being adopted and both having Downs Syndrome. Life had been beautiful until I was twelve when my parents both died in a freak airplane accident. After my brothers were placed in group homes, I was sent to live with a maiden aunt who had no interest in raising a teenager. She was fifteen years older than me and spent most of her nights drunk or high, a revolving door of boyfriends parading through the house.

Tragedy is not an uncommon story and I was certainly grateful for the first twelve years of my life. At age 17 I moved out, finished high school at night and worked dayshift at a local supermarket. I finally landed a job as a telemarketer at a local advertising agency after I graduated. The stadium had been my weekend job.

At the age of twenty-four, I was only now in a place financially where I could start to think about furthering my education. I had already applied to the local community college and was just waiting to see if I would be eligible for financial aid before officially registering for classes.

Mr. Talcos' voice intruded on my thoughts.

"He was a good man."

Startled I looked over. He continued to stare at the waves while I waited for him to explain.

"His whole life. He was a good man."

He turned toward me and from the far away look in his eyes, I realized he wasn't really seeing me but I knew he was talking about Declan.

"He was," I said. "Looking back, I don't know exactly what spurred me to help him but I'm pretty sure it had something to do with feeling that he was a good man."

Mr. Talcos' eyes focused and he nodded, silently agreeing.

I stopped talking but my thoughts kept going. Maybe there was a deeper reason, one I didn't entirely understand. Certainly, as we stood facing each other the night he appeared in the stadium bathroom, something in me answered something in him. I knew he needed me. Did he need me now?

Stepping back from the rail, I told Mr. Talcos that dinner was ready and invited him to come eat. I waited while he moved away from where he leant and walked behind him toward the house. I followed his listless gait, reaching around to slide the door open for him.

Adam met us in the hall; a dark lock of hair falling into his eyes before he tiredly wiped it back across his forehead.

"Mr. Talcos, Aimee," he said, "we're heading out, but I need to caution you not to go into the study and not to touch anything. We've locked up the room for now. I'm going down to the station. Once the medical examiner is done, we'll let you know where you can have the funeral home pick-up the body."

I blanched. Declan's face once again came to my mind at the mention of the body. I must have looked like I was going to faint because Adam reached out a hand and carefully took my arm, pulling me into the kitchen and helping me into a chair. Mr. Talcos stood by looking helpless.

"I apologize," Adam said, as he straightened up from helping me sit, "I might have been too blunt."

He looked over at Mr. Talcos, "I'll come over tomorrow morning to discuss arrangements with you. Do you think the two of you will be okay tonight?"

Declan's grandfather assured him that we would be fine and walked him to the front door. As I breathed in and out, I could feel my body relaxing and the dizziness in my head clearing.

Standing slowly, I tested out my legs before moving to take the food out of the oven. I shakily managed to pour and place glasses of iced tea on the table with little more than a small spill on the counter. I was just getting seated when Mr. Talcos joined me.

## Chapter 6

"You loved him."

The gruff voice reverberated around the room. I looked up in surprise from where I sat across the kitchen table. Mr. Talcos' plate was clean and he sat observing me with half-closed eyes.

For the past five minutes we had eaten in silence. Since I had already told him the entire story, his comment seemed to come from left field.

My mouth full of potato, I chewed and swallowed slowing, trying to form an answer.

"I trusted him. I don't know that I would say I lov…" my voice trailed off.

"Yes?" he asked, leaning towards me.

I frowned, "It was all rather sudden."

He nodded encouragingly.

Looking back at my plate, I stabbed another home fry with my fork. "Impulsive, actually. He needed help and I wanted to help him."

"You felt strongly for him."

Why was everyone was so quick to assume they knew my feelings for Declan when even I was unsure? Rather than contradict him, I smiled at the old gentleman, feeling a sense of *déja vu* as I realized his eyes were the same shape and almost the same color as his grandson's.

My smile faltered and I needed to change the subject. Fast. I did not want to talk about my motives for helping Declan and especially not about my feelings for him.

So I brought up the lock box.

"The police say the safe in the study was broken into and possibly robbed. It was wide open and there was nothing inside. Do you think maybe a thief surprised Declan while he was working in the study?"

Mr. Talcos shrugged his shoulders, letting me change the subject.

"Could be," he said rather vaguely. "No one was supposed to be here."

Even though I hadn't made my mind up about whether or not I wanted to get involved, I found myself asking curiously, "What exactly was in the safe?"

His lips pursed.

For a moment I thought he might not divulge the secret, but then he spoke, "There was a considerable amount of money, for one thing. At least five thousand dollars. There was also a copy of my will, some jewelry that belonged to my late wife and also a couple things from Declan's mother."

He hesitated a moment before shrugging and saying, "Also some business papers but I can't imagine that would interest anyone who isn't directly involved in company stuff."

"What company?" I asked, my interest immediately aroused. Were we talking about the same business that Declan was accused of embezzling?

Mr. Talcos cleared his throat before answering. "My company and Declan's company, Autem Viris."

He picked up his fork and tapped his plate with it. I watched the repetitive action distractedly while he went on.

"I started it over fifty years ago. Initially I built a research institution with funding from MIT but over the years it grew into an international bioresearch firm. Right now we're creating a vaccine for the Zika virus, among other things. You might have seen it on the news."

I could tell that he was proud of his accomplishments and rightfully so. Though I hadn't heard of his company before, I had heard about the upcoming release of the vaccine.

"That's where Declan worked? For you?"

He stopped tapping and put his fork down to stare at me.

"Worked for me? Declan possessed more than half the shares of that company, all passed on from his parents."

The news report had been sadly lacking in details.

"I didn't know."

Mr. Talcos frowned. "Yes, that's where he worked, for fourteen years. I hired him right out of college and watched as he climbed his way to the top. When I retired six years ago, I left the firm in his capable hands."

His grey eyes unfocused as he continued, "He may have inherited his share of the profits but he earned his position. Declan never once took advantage of being my grandson. He was the manager and CEO of Autem Viris because he worked hard to get there. He was loyal to me and our company."

"So what do you think happened?" I asked, completely abandoning any pretense I had of not concerning myself with Declan's business.

Mr. Talcos focused on me again. "They found three billion dollars missing, that's what happened."

I knew that. At least, I had known he was accused of embezzling money from his company. But three billion dollars? That was a lot of money.

Mr. Talcos watched my reaction.

"You didn't know about this?" he asked, reaching for the fork he had just laid down.

*Please don't tap that again*, I thought while I shook my head in the negative.

Thankfully he pushed it under the edge of his plate.

"No, I knew he was wanted for embezzlement, but not of his own company. Declan never told me why we were running. I found out when I saw it on the news the night before, he...um..." I gulped, "died."

I had broached the subject with Declan the evening after I had seen the news spot. It had been little more than a flash, really, saying that Declan Talcos was still being hunted by the FBI but not much more. He had been uncommunicative, asking me to continue to trust him. We had gone to our separate rooms and except for pouring him a cup of coffee and bringing it into the study the next morning, I hadn't seen him again until I found him dead.

"Can you tell me about it?" I inquired hesitantly, lest I sound pushy.

Declan's grandfather scooted his chair away from the table and then settled back into it. I could tell he was reminiscing before he answered. "I think to understand what happened, you need to understand a little more about Declan."

His eyes met mine and I gave a small nod, encouraging him to continue and at the same time, acknowledging that I really hadn't known his grandson.

"Declan was my only grandson. His parents, my son and his wife, died in a car accident when he was nine, leaving him and his sister, Elyse, alone. She was just two at the time. My wife and I immediately applied and were granted guardianship."

He sighed and I guessed he was thinking about his deceased wife.

"From an early age," he went on, "Declan showed promise. He was smart, ambitious and hard working. His father had never shown an interest in bioresearch and, especially after his death, my hope grew that someday Declan would take over the company for me."

Hearing praise of Declan made me smile and it seemed that these memories lifted Mr. Talcos' spirits as well.

His face relaxed and he continued, "He graduated from Stanford with a bachelors in research and finished his MBA one year later at Harvard. I immediately hired him into the company but only as an entry-level researcher. Over the next seven years he worked his way up to management and by the time I was ready to retire and hand over the company, I was confident he was ready to the job."

Mr. Talcos shifted in his seat and I realized the hard kitchen chair was probably getting uncomfortable. I fleetingly thought about offering to move to the living room but he continued talking.

"Declan didn't prove me wrong. Six years ago when I retired, the firm didn't have three billion dollars to embezzle. The fact that he took a multi-million dollar company and turned it into a multi-billion dollar corporation is no small feat."

He spoke with pride but also love.

"And he never married?" I asked, realizing I had never thought to ask Declan that question. I remembered finding out his age on our wedding day. He hadn't looked thirty-five years old, at least not to me. This made him almost eleven years older than me. My surprised expression when he wrote his birth year on the wedding license application had made him laugh. That had been one of the few opportunities we had found that day for levity.

"He might have come close once or twice," mused Mr. Talcos, unperturbed by my question, "but he never tied the knot. Of course, when his sister Elyse died he seemed to withdraw from everyone socially and really threw himself into the company."

"His sister died?"

"Yes, five years ago."

"How did she die?" I asked in a small voice, my heart beginning to pound. For no reason at all I began to feel anxious.

Mr. Talcos' face saddened and I realized it was hard for him to talk about the loss of his only granddaughter.

"The three of us were boating off the coast of Yarmouth when we were hit with a sudden squall and the boat sprung a leak. Declan tried to rescue his sister but it was all he could do to get himself to shore. He reentered the water when he saw me struggling and helped me the last thirty or so yards. By the time we were both safely on land, there was no sign of Elyse. Rescue boats were dispatched but of course, by then, it was too late."

My heart ached for Declan in that moment, imagining him standing on the shore in the wind and rain, looking for and not seeing his only sister. I couldn't imagine the guilt and misery that must have consumed him after he had failed to rescue her.

Then I looked at Mr. Talcos and my heart ached for him as well. I could see that he still harbored pain from losing his granddaughter so tragically. I could only imagine how much more sorrow he felt now, compounded by the murder of his grandson.

"When did your wife die?" I asked, and not very tactfully I might add.

It seemed to pull Mr. Talcos from his painful memories.

"About ten years ago. She died of cancer."

I swallowed; shocked by the amount of tragedy this family had already been dealt.

Looking at the weary old man before me, I suddenly felt the need to comfort him.

"You don't think Declan had anything to do with this embezzlement, do you?" I asked pleadingly, not wanting him to carry the burden of believing his only grandson had turned on him in his last hour.

Mr. Talcos took a moment to answer and when he did I saw the deep sadness in the lines of his face, "I don't know what to think. I don't want to believe he was guilty and yet, no one else could have taken the money, according to the FBI."

I heard what he said and knew there was more to the story. I wanted to demand how they could know this with such certitude but I let it go.

Standing, I grabbed my grandfather-in-law's plate and put it on top of mine, clearing the table. As I took his glass and looked down at his crestfallen expression, I knew I had to say something.

Lifting my chin, I gazed steadily at him until he looked up.

With a firm voice, I said, "Declan told me he was innocent. I don't know what the true story is but you can be confident that he didn't betray you."

Mr. Talcos' eyes filled with tears and his voice broke as he responded barely above a whisper, "Thank you, Aimee."

I carried the dishes over to the sink. Turning on the faucet, I let the water run until it was hot. Moments later as I began scrubbing, I sensed rather than saw Mr. Talcos leave the room.

## Chapter 7

The next morning Adam returned, just as he had said, to discuss burial plans with us. Since I was more spectator than anything else during the conversation, I found my thoughts wandering.

First I noticed how serious Adam looked, his strong, chiseled jaw shadowed as if he hadn't yet found time to shave following the events of the day before. Taller than even Declan, he towered over Mr. Talcos and me. But where Declan had been weighed down by his troubles, Adam looked ready to take on the world.

Quickly banishing my thoughts, I felt a twinge of guilt for even noticing Adam in relation to Declan. I tried to refocus on what the two men were saying.

It appeared they both wanted to have a quiet graveside service, forgoing an obituary notice, wake or calling hours. They had a desire to avoid media attention and I could understand their reasons for performing the burial before the news of Declan's death was released. The last person I wanted to see at the cemetery was someone with a news camera.

The only thing holding us up at this point was the medical examiner's autopsy, which Adam reassured us would be done within the next day or two. Mr. Talcos, after politely soliciting my input, arranged for the funeral to take place at a local cemetery in three days, pending the pathologist releasing the body.

As I sat there listening to their low-voiced discussion, it struck me for a second time that I would never see Declan again. It didn't matter what I had or hadn't felt for him. I would never have the opportunity to get to know him. The man who had waltzed into my life, asked me to drop everything, and then relied on my discretion and ability to trust him was gone.

Following this train of thought, I think I kind of checked out for the rest of the conversation. The men arranged all the details while I sat trying not to feel, their voices like background noise to my melancholy thoughts.

When they finished, Adam took my hand, looked me over searchingly, and asked me to call him if I had any concerns. He promised to be in touch over the next two days with the examiner's report and to check on us. I nodded, barely taking in what he said.

After he left, a cold and vulnerable feeling crowded my heart. I felt very lonely. I wondered how concerned Adam could really be for my well-being. I had to be the main suspect in the eyes of the police. After all, I was the only person who knew where Declan was these past two weeks. And if they thought he was making off with billions of dollars, who was the most logical person to know where that money was hidden? His widow, of course, and that would be me. And if they suspected someone of killing him for that money? Again, me.

The fear of being accused of Declan's death chilled me thoroughly and the anxiety from yesterday returned in full force.

Two days later we had the results. The medical examiner's report was straightforward and didn't tell us anything we hadn't already figured out. Declan was killed with a shot to the head and died instantly. No drugs, legal or otherwise, were found in his system. Time of death was determined to be within an hour of the body being discovered.

The FBI, or rather some men in suits, came by to interview me about my time with Declan. I assumed they were with the FBI since all of their questions had to do with my recent association and subsequent marriage to Declan. Our conversation lasted several hours and left me feeling incompetent as I repeatedly told them "I don't know."

I also found out that I was inexplicably lucky. It would have been an impossible task to prove I hadn't killed Declan but for one small detail. Several years prior, Mr. Talcos had installed a security camera in the rear of the house following an incident with a vandal. The culprit had spray-painted the back of the house and thrown his deck chairs around.

In an effort to prevent a recurrence, a professional security company had been called in and a camera installed overlooking the back of the house. Thankfully their footage recorded me on tape all morning, reading and taking in the ocean scene. This provided me an alibi since I never left the deck until Declan's grandfather found me.

Mr. Talcos also had a witness to verify his story. The taxi driver who dropped him off at the house was located fairly easily as Mr. Talcos used him routinely. It was easy to prove that he had been dropped off only momentarily before he found me on his back porch because he paid the driver with a credit card, which had a time stamp. It certainly was not enough time to kill his grandson and stuff him under a desk.

All in all, I considered us extremely blessed to have sound alibis. Adam apparently thought so too as he told us more than once that we were luckier than most people. As Mr. Talcos had just lost a grandson and I, my husband, I thought this was not entirely true but I didn't say anything. I knew what he meant.

Later that day, as Adam was leaving, I broached another matter with him: what I was going to wear to the funeral. It might be a silly concern, but it was also a legitimate one. I obviously had very few things with me. Declan and I had stopped once in a small, out of the way drugstore for toiletries and I had bought some extra jeans and tee shirts at a thrift store but otherwise I had nothing to wear, especially to a funeral.

"Adam," I called out, catching his attention as he opened the front door. I had followed him out of the living room, leaving Mr. Talcos perusing the official coroner's report.

"Can we talk for a second?"

He turned and looked me over before nodding and starting to shut the door.

"How about outside?" I asked, stepping towards him, feeling shy. Swinging the door wide open, he gestured for me to precede him. I stepped past him onto the white wooden flooring of the front porch, looking for a place to sit.

The overhang provided shade over half the area but with a cool breeze coming off the water, I chose to sit in a chair in direct sunlight. Adam joined me at the far end of the deck, perching awkwardly on a rickety wooden bench.  I could tell he had no clue why I wanted to speak with him and it made him curious. Ironically, it made me even more nervous.

Avoiding his searching gaze, I dove in, my words tripping over themselves, "I have a bit of a problem. I'm not allowed to leave the house; but, quite frankly, I have nothing appropriate with me for a funeral. All I have are the clothes I'm wearing and another pair of jeans and some blouses. They're not even black."

Understanding dawned in his eyes and I continued rather determinedly, "If I could be permitted to go shopping for maybe an hour or so, I'm sure I could find something quickly."

His mouth quirked in a smile and he replied, "Not a problem. If you're free to go now, I'll escort you to the mall and we can be back before I need to report in to the station."

"A police escort? To go shopping?"

He laughed lightly, "Yep."

"I have my own car," I pointed my index finger at the driveway, indicating my old beater sitting in the shade.

"It's for your own protection," he insisted as he stood, "and unless you'd rather have a female cop, I have no problem standing outside a store for half an hour while you find something."

I bit my lip. Shopping was probably not exactly his thing but I could find something quickly. Agreeing before I had a chance to change my mind, I turned and rushed into the house. I hurried upstairs to grab my purse and let Mr. Talcos know where we were going before running back to Adam who stood patiently just off the porch, cell phone in hand.

He waited until I reached the bottom of the steps, then turned and walked me toward his car. Thankfully his vehicle looked like a normal car and not a police cruiser. I think seeing lights and gadgets would have scared me back into the house.

To my chagrin, he accompanied me to the passenger's side and opened the front door. After making sure I was completely tucked in, he shut the door and walked around to climb in on the other side.

Aware I was with a cop, I made a show of putting on my seatbelt. I peeked at him after it clicked and caught him checking his phone one more time. Glancing at me, he apologized and then slipped it into the front pocket of his button-down shirt before starting the car. I sat back and tried to take a calming breath, unsure why I was so besought by nerves. I slowly exhaled, willing myself not to be aware of how close he was or how small the car seemed with him next to me.

As we rode into town, Adam attempted to make small talk about the weather, the town and other inconsequential subjects. If he was trying to make me feel comfortable, his plan backfired. I had trouble coming up with a response to the simplest questions and cringed over half the things I said.

A few times the police scanner went off and a static voice came across, loud and disruptive. By the third time it was clear that Adam and I had run out of things to talk about. I watched as trees passed by, their branches reaching over the road like arms. We pulled into a small indoor mall with several brand labels written across the front.

It embarrassed me that I couldn't hold a casual conversation with Adam. The scanner had quieted down and as we parked, an awkward silence lay between us.

I beat him getting out of the car but he caught up and held the glass door to the mall open for me as we entered. Then he asked where I wanted to go, reading off the few department stores listed in the directory and locating the store I picked out.

I was bothered by Adam's courtesy. I'm not sure why it annoyed me, but it did. As he walked at my side, I was tempted to ask if he was always this attentive or if he only treated suspects with this much consideration. I stopped, as I realized I was being unduly sensitive and that my attitude was bordering on rude.

When we reached the department store, Adam followed me to the clothing section and then stood back. He remained at a distance with his feet apart and arms crossed like a bodyguard, but at least he allowed me some privacy. I could still see him out of the corner of my eye as I flipped through the clearance section in the back of the dress department, hoping to find something as quickly as possible. My hand lit on three black dresses hung side by side and since they all appeared appropriate for a funeral, I grabbed them and ducked into a fitting room to try them on.

The first one made me look fat, or at least feel like I looked fat, something I often dealt with being only 5'2". When you put on a dress meant for someone with long legs and instead of going to your knees it hits you mid-calf, well, it never looks flattering.

Taking it off, I tried on the next one. It made me look like a grandmother. The black lace covering the bodice reached up to create a high neck and just putting it on gave me a choking sensation.

I finally settled for the third dress, not because I looked great in it but rather because I was starting to feel guilty for caring at all how I looked when I was going to my husband's funeral. It had a full A-line skirt that settled just below my knees and the capped sleeves and square neckline were modest.

We checked out at the front, Adam waiting for me in the doorway. He smiled as I approached and then gestured for me to walk beside him.

"How did you pay for that?" he asked as I reshouldered my purse.

I bristled, not liking the question.

"With my money."

"Credit card?"

"No, cash. Why?"

"Just curious. Was it money Declan gave you?"

I felt my face turn red and I stopped.

"Declan did not give me any money. Everything I have with me is money I earned."

"Okay." Adam's expression was difficult to read. "Where to next?"

His tone was accommodating and I looked at him suspiciously.

"Maybe some shoes?" I suggested, slightly confused by his quick change of subject. One second I felt like I was being interrogated, and the next, taken care of by a friend.

"Lead the way," he said and I turned to start walking.

We had passed a shoe store when we first came in, so I strolled back towards it.

I picked out a pair of black pumps and then, declining Adam's reluctant offer to stop for lunch in the food court, we exited the mall.

Approaching the car, Adam opened the front passenger door of his grey unmarked vehicle, taking my bags and putting them in the back seat. He waited until I was situated and then closed the door.

With one hand on the seatbelt, I watched him go around the front of the car and grudgingly noticed he cut a handsome figure with his slender height and confident stride. As he settled into the driver's seat beside me, the front compartment of the vehicle suddenly felt even more claustrophobic than before.

Clumsily reaching for the buckle, I snapped my seatbelt in place. Then I turned to gaze out the window, trying to focus on anything but the man beside me. Our ride home was even quieter than it had been on the way in.

## Chapter 8

Declan's funeral was held early Friday morning as planned. Mr. Talcos and I drove in a rented limo, escorted by the police. We arrived just as the ceremony commenced, the sky overcast and ominous. A priest stood at the graveside, blessing the casket with holy water and conducting the burial rites in a low tone.

I kept my eyes to the ground, except for a few surreptitious glances at the handful of strangers aligned along the opposite side of the casket.

Since there were four or five other people at the funeral, I assumed Mr. Talcos invited them. One couple in particular stood out. They had arrived late and stood directly across from us. It had taken only a glance to recognize that the woman was unusually beautiful. She had dark, velvet-smooth hair and a creamy complexion that would rival any skin product commercial. Her eyes, almost violet, were full of tears and I could see dark shadows underneath as she dabbed at them with a handkerchief provided by the man at her side.

He was also strikingly good-looking and I couldn't help but think what a handsome couple they made. Her boyfriend, or maybe her husband, stood erectly at her side, his arm supporting her, looking just as solemn.

My attention shifted and I gazed at the simple wooden box that was Declan's final resting place. Images of his face under the desk passed before me and I fought unsuccessfully to erase them. I must have made a whimper because Mr. Talcos took my hand and threaded it through his arm, resting his fingers over my slightly trembling ones.

The wind began to pick up and the service concluded just as the first drop of rain fell. Initially it was a light drizzle and I ignored it. I wanted to stay and see the casket lowered, but as the rain became heavier, I felt Mr. Talcos press my arm and incline his head in the direction of the waiting vehicles. Someone handed me an open black umbrella and as a crack of thunder rumbled across the sky I followed Declan's grandfather to the rented black limo, trying to keep both of us covered.

As we began the drive home I thought about the past two and a half weeks with Declan. The time had flown by quickly and yet each moment was engraved in my memory like his name would soon be on his headstone.

He had been so distant and unapproachable and yet at the same time kind and considerate. He had remained calm and upbeat through the stress of hiding, hours of driving, and uncomfortable nights sleeping in the car, a campsite or cheap hotel. I had never seen him angry. Worried and tired maybe, but never angry.

I glanced at my grandfather-in-law who was lost in his own thoughts and it occurred to me how unusual and sad it was that Declan had spent the last two weeks of his life with a perfect stranger, and even more oddly, that the stranger was me.

A memory came as we zoomed down the highway, rain pounding a steady rhythm above us. The day after we'd arrived in Little Rock, Declan had come up behind me in our hotel room. His proximity had always made me nervous and I startled slightly as his hand came down to lightly rest on my shoulder.

I turned and our eyes met.

"Aimee," he began, his gaze sincere and searching, "I have something I need to say."

A jittery, apprehensive feeling went through me.

"I want you to know that I am not taking you for granted. I'm between a rock and a hard place and having you here is making this just a little easier for me."

He took a deep breath as if gunning for courage. "I know it would be better for you if we separated but I'm too selfish to force you to leave."

The nervous bubble inside me deflated slightly. He wasn't making me depart.

Declan's shoulders set resolutely as he continued, "I'm not too selfish to tell you that you should go. It's the right thing to do."

Suddenly the limo took a sharp turn, bringing me back to the present. Mr. Talcos was caught off guard and slid into the door. I grabbed the seat and held on as we turned off the exit ramp. Straightening out again, we entered a tree-lined street heading toward town and my thoughts drifted back to Declan.

I now recognized Declan's valiant attempt to give me the chance to escape; to flee his criminal charges, the difficulties of living on the run and also the unknown dangers associated with his personal quest, whatever that may have been.

In an attempt to push away what I perceived as rejection, I remember telling him defiantly, "Sorry but unless you're abandoning me here in Arkansas, you're stuck with me."

He hadn't laughed in return or even smiled. Instead he'd contemplated me silently and I had embarrassedly turned away.

The limo hit a bump and I was jarred from my thoughts again. We were nearing the center of town, only ten minutes from the house. Declan's plot was an hour away, chosen by Mr. Talcos for reasons unknown to me.

Not many people had been invited to the funeral owing to the fact that the police wanted to keep Declan's death from the media and the public eye. I personally hadn't invited anyone. My two roommates, the only people who would care if I went missing, thought I was taking a vacation and my boss thought I was sick.

I thought of the couple I had noticed earlier. When the service ended, the woman had turned toward the man with a loud wail. He held her tightly while she sobbed, her shoulders shaking in grief. Guiltily I had averted my eyes, realizing she was showing more emotion than I was, and I was Declan's widow.

Now, I began to wonder who she was. I broke the silence we had ridden with since leaving the cemetery and asked my grandfather-in-law, "Mr. Talcos, who was the woman who was crying at the funeral?"

Mr. Talcos blinked at me uncomprehendingly. I had obviously disturbed him in his own train of thought.

I blushed slightly, knowing that once again I had blurted a question without thinking, but continued to press, "The woman who stood across from us, with the dark hair. She was very beautiful. Was she a friend of Declan's?"

Mr. Talcos' eyes cleared in understanding. "Oh, yes. That's Alyssa. She and Declan were high school sweethearts. They broke up to go to different colleges and then dated briefly again after they graduated. They broke up permanently shortly after Declan's sister died and Alyssa ended up marrying Declan's best friend, Erik. Alyssa and Eric are both employees of Autem Viris, my company."

His voice was matter-of-fact and I couldn't tell if it had been an amiable break-up or not.

"That was Erik with her?" I clarified, feeling nosey as I attempted to find out yet another detail of Declan's personal life. Had there been hard feelings between Erik and Declan after Erik had married his ex-girlfriend?

"Yes, eclan met Erik in college. I contacted Erik a couple days ago. I knew, even with everything that's happened, they'd want to be there."

At first I thought by everything he must mean the breakup and subsequent marriage but then I remembered Declan was wanted by the law and now murdered.

Mr. Talcos left it at that and I turned to look out my window at the pouring rain. Something in my heart clenched and I couldn't stop myself from thinking jealously that Declan must have loved her; Alyssa was so beautiful.

Quick to perish the thought, I reminded myself that Declan's and my relationship had been unique. There was no way anyone could compare it to a traditional marriage. As if to reassure myself, I told myself that he may not have loved me, but he had needed me. And it was becoming apparent that at some level, I had needed him as well.

"He never loved her," Mr. Talcos broke in to my thoughts, as if he could read my mind. I turned back from the window to look at him questioningly.

"He tried, but for the most part, she was like a sister. Most people believe that she broke things off with him in order to pursue a relationship with Erik, but the truth is Declan broke up with her first."

I blushed and turned away, not sure how to answer him, not sure what he was reading on my face.

We arrived home to a thunderously quiet house. The pounding of the ocean waves and the driving rain on the roof drowned out all the normal sounds I usually took for granted: the ticking of the clock, the hum of the refrigerator and the buzz of the fan.

I slowly made my way upstairs. It was only eleven in the morning but it was dark, the clouds and rain making it feel like dusk was settling in. Between the funeral and not sleeping well, I felt completely drained. If only I could go to bed and wake up like nothing had ever happened.

With a sense of relief I slowly pushed open my bedroom door, reaching out to flick on the light. As I entered, I looked up and stifled a gasp. All thoughts of sleep fled as I took in the scene before me.

My room was in shambles. The drawers from the dresser were pulled out and dumped on the floor. The sheets and blankets had been ripped from the bed and were puddled at the foot of it while the mattress itself was standing on end. My clothing and personal belongings were scattered along the floor and I saw that my bathroom door was half open with the light on.

Quickly back-pedaling from the room, I called out to Mr. Talcos, unable to mask the panic and fear in my voice.

He arrived as quickly as his aging body would allow and after one quick glance inside, he calmly told me to call the police. Without crossing into the room, he leaned forward and grabbed the handle, swinging the wooden door closed.

Pulling my phone from my purse, I tried to get my fingers to follow my brain's commands. I started to dial 911 but then stopped. Maybe this wasn't an emergency. No one was hurt. Should I really bother the people dealing with car accidents and heart attacks? On the other hand, what if the intruder was still in the house?

I glanced down the dim hall, deciding. I did have Adam's number in my purse.

I deleted the numbers 9 and 1, and pulled Adam's card from my wallet. Dialing in the phone number written beneath his name, I shifted my weight from one leg to the other. Was I doing the right thing?

After the fourth ring I was ready to hang up and just dial 911. Then I heard a mechanical pause and Adam's voice coming through, "Detective Harrison speaking."

"Adam?" I asked, suddenly nervous that I shouldn't have called, "It's Aimee. Do you think you could come to the house? We appear to have had a break in."

Adam's voice came through strong and concerned, "Are you okay? Are you safe?"

I looked over at Mr. Talcos who was listening intently. "I think we're okay but we just arrived home and I don't know if the intruder is still here. I found my bedroom torn up. I don't know what the other rooms look like."

Adam said something under his breath before coming back through the line, "Are you near a bathroom? I want you to lock yourselves inside."

I looked at Mr. Talcos, "He says we need to lock ourselves in the nearest bathroom. Should we go into my bedroom's bathroom?"

Mr. Talcos shook his head and started walking away, "There's one toward the front of the house. Let's stay out of your bedroom for now."

I talked back into the mouthpiece. "Okay, we're locking ourselves in the upstairs bathroom." I looked around before following Mr. Talcos inside, "It's to the right at the top of the stairs."

"Good. A police officer should be there shortly. Don't touch anything, not even the doorknob, if you can help it. I want you stay on the phone with me until the police come up and let you out."

We'd already touched the bedroom doorknob but I figured we could tell him that later. Pulling the phone away from my ear I relayed the message to Mr. Talcos. Then we sat with my phone on speaker, listening to

Adam's scanner go off every once in a while as he drove.

Thankfully the bathroom faced the front of the house and had a small window. We watched outside as a police car with two officers pulled up almost immediately. Adam was only a minute behind them and by the look on his face I could see he was worried. He jumped out of his car and met the other two behind their car. They huddled for a few minutes before cautiously going off in different directions. Adam came directly toward the front of the house.

I realized he must have put me on mute while he was talking to the other officers because at this point I heard Adam speak again.

"Aimee? I'm going to clear the house and then come find you. Do not leave the bathroom."

Relieved they had finally arrived I found myself choking down a giggle in response. Several minutes later, a knock came at the door.

"Aimee? Mr. Talcos? It's Adam. It's safe to come out."

I wanted to rush out of the room and jump into his arms, safety suddenly more attractive than anything I had yet witnessed in him, but I held back. Adam's expression as we filed out was serious and he searched our faces before asking us to follow him downstairs to the living room.

Once inside, he asked us to tell him how we had discovered the break-in. I told him my side and then looked out through the window as Mr. Talcos explained his part. The outlines of the two officers were visible through the sheer curtains hanging from the rod. I watched as more bodies ascended the porch steps and shortly thereafter a head popped into the room and a uniformed officer waved Adam over.

After speaking to the man in hushed tones, Adam asked us to wait while he went upstairs. Upon his return, he asked me specifically to accompany him and tell him if anything was missing from my bedroom.

The idea of someone stealing my belongings made me scoff. I possessed nothing of value. However, to be obliging I went upstairs and looked around the ransacked room. The top mattress had been returned to its place and I quickly bent over to collect the clothing littering the ground. The drawers were back in the dresser but still open. Laying things out on the bed, I went through them without finding even one missing sock.

Adam watched me as I went through my stuff. Then he indicated the bathroom with one hand while stepping closer. "I want you to check in the bathroom, too, but I have to warn you; there is a message written on the mirror. Did you see it earlier?"

My eyes must have widened because he put his hand on my upper arm as if to steady me.

"I didn't think so," was all he said, gently squeezing and letting go before stepping away. I bravely walked in front of him the fifteen or so steps toward the half open door and peered in.

It was a pretty decent-sized bathroom. The tub and shower fit along one wall with a vanity counter and the sink on the other side. All the overhead lights were on and an officer was on his hands and knees, scraping something from the tile in front of the toilet.

That however wasn't what caught my attention. Written on the mirror, in huge, white letters, were the words, "You can't hide forever!" punctuated with a large X at the bottom.

I had been scared before but now I positively panicked. All I could think was I needed to get away. I knew without a doubt that someone deliberately searched my room and left that message for me.

Turning, I ran from the room, down the stairs and had the front door open before Adam caught up to me.

"Aimee! Wait!"

He grasped my shoulders and I found myself shaking and breathing hard as I came to an abrupt stop. Slowly he released me and turned me toward him. Our eyes locked and I froze in place. He said nothing and I said nothing until I bent over double, breaking the hold he had on me. I stayed like that until my respirations returned to normal.

"You should sit down," he said as I lifted my head. He took my hand and led me through the still open entranceway. I sank gratefully onto one of the benches that flanked the front door and bent forward, this time slowing my breathing with conscious intention.

The cool sea breeze and the sound of seagulls penetrated my mind as I calmed down. All was quiet as I regained my composure and I realized that Adam was waiting.

"I should have given you more warning," he began apologetically as my eyes met his.

I gave him a wan smile before looking down at my hands gripped tightly in my lap. I took another long shaking breath and deliberately unclasped my fingers.

"How could you have known I would react like that?" I asked, shaking my head, "I don't even know why I reacted like that."

Adam cleared his throat and I could almost hear a smile in his voice as he answered, "Well, maybe it's because you just spent two weeks on the run from the law. You married a perfect stranger and three days later found him murdered. Then you found out you're implicated in a federal investigation for an embezzlement you weren't aware occurred and now, when all you want is a day to mourn and bury your husband, you discover your room wrecked and a threatening message written on your mirror."

I stared at him a moment, bug-eyed.

"Yep, that might be why."

His eyes crinkled in amusement and I found myself sniffling and offering a weak smile in return.

Strangely enough, hearing all the terrible things of the past few weeks said in one breath made it suddenly more bearable.

"Not to mention that I'm scared to death I'm going to be arrested as an accessory and spend the next gazillion years in prison," I offered, starting to regain my composure.

Adam handed me a tissue and I blew my nose.

"I did mention you are being investigated for a crime you didn't know was committed," he said teasingly.

I frowned, still serious. "Being investigated is nothing like the fear of being convicted."

He smiled. "Aimee, the crime happened before you were in the picture. As long as you stick around and we can't find any ties between you and three billion dollars, you're going to be okay."

His face became serious. "Stop worrying. We'll get to the bottom of this."

I looked up from the tissue and sniffled, "Before or after I serve my time?"

"That's positive thinking," he grinned, looking up as another officer came out on the porch. He rose to speak with him.

"We're done with the second room," the officer reported. "We're going to get all this stuff back to the lab. Is there anything else you need before we go?"

Adam stepped inside the house to give last minute instructions, my brain registering that there was a second room that had been searched by the intruder.

Adam returned and his quiet gaze met mine as he quietly shut the front door behind him.

"A second room?"

"It was the room that Declan slept in," he said matter-of-factly. "Less roughed up than yours and no spray paint on the mirror either."

I bit my lip, a little lost as to why someone would break into the house and destroy our rooms, let alone leave threatening messages.

"They didn't touch Mr. Talcos' room?"

"Not that we can tell. Any idea what they were looking for?"

Realizing Adam wanted my input, I hurried to say, "No, not really. I don't have anything of value and you guys already went through Declan's stuff after he died."

My voice rose as I finished my declaration and I closed my eyes, trying to calm myself back down. It was embarrassingly easy to flip back into panic mode.

"Is there anything Declan left with you? Or maybe gave you?"

I shook my head, "No."

"Not even a wedding ring."

It was a statement more than a question. I opened my eyes and realized Adam was looking directly at my ring finger from where he stood. I changed the position of my hands to cover my naked digit.

"Was he planning on buying you one?" he asked, his tone curious.

I shifted in my chair uncomfortably. "I don't know. We never talked about it."

Adam moved to sit beside me on the bench and I turned away from him. He didn't seem to notice.

"Can you think back again, Aimee? Did Declan ever give you anything, maybe something you wouldn't associate as being important? Something he wanted you to put in your purse or hold onto for him? Or maybe something he meant to ask for later?"

I shook my head adamantly. I knew that Adam was trying to get to the bottom of this but he was barking up the wrong tree.

"Really there was nothing, not even a tic tac."

Adam pulled out his notebook and started to write.

"So what now?" I asked, after we sat in silence a little longer than I was comfortable with.

"Well, it appears less than likely you were involved in the break-in since you were under surveillance during the funeral and throughout the entire morning."

He leaned back and stretched out his long legs. I nodded in response, taking him seriously until he turned to look down at me and I saw the twinkle in his eyes. He was teasing me.

"And you have an alibi for the morning of the murder."

I grimaced.

"So I'd say things look pretty good on the arrest front," he went on, "but now you appear to be threatened by someone. So while you are not under house arrest, for your protection, I think you need to stay here under police custody, at least for a little while."

He lifted an eyebrow at me. "This is for your safety."

"This means I can't go anywhere alone?"

He nodded, looking back out over the railing. "Or leave town. If you're not in the house, I need to know exactly where you are."

I promptly acquiesced to his rules, grateful to have the house restriction lifted. Honestly, after today I would be scared to death to go anywhere alone anyway.

"Does this mean I'm no longer a suspect?" I asked, more out of curiosity than anything else.

Adam pulled his legs back beneath him and stood, "Until we catch the killer, everyone is suspect." He turned toward me. "We still don't have a reason for what happened today. I'm not trying to scare you but I want you to be careful."

Knowing the person who had left the message in my bathroom was possibly nearby, even at this exact moment, was enough to make me hole up in my bedroom, with the doors locked and the windows nailed shut, for weeks. It occurred to me that I really wasn't a brave person.

Adam seemed to understand my fears and after patting my shoulder awkwardly, he headed into the house.

As I sat there, staring distractedly at the deck chairs on the opposite end, it occurred to me that now more than ever I believed Declan was innocent of the embezzlement charges. His murder somehow tied into his alleged crime.

Logic said if Declan hadn't stolen the money, then someone else had. The FBI, according to Mr. Talcos, thought they had inviolable proof that Declan was the thief. That being said, someone must have used Declan to embezzle the money and if that were the case, maybe there was still something of Declan's that they needed to access the money. And they thought I had it.

## Chapter 9

"Am I interrupting your solitude?" A deep voice broke through the morning quiet as I sat watching the waves while sipping my first cup of joe for the day. I almost spilled my coffee. It momentarily brought me back to the time Mr. Talcos and I first met, but this wasn't the voice of my grandfather-in-law.

Turning, I saw Adam standing behind me. I had been aimlessly staring at the ocean, the steady roll of the surf blocking out his approach and the early morning sun warming my skin. Unsure of the time, I surreptitiously glanced at my phone screen.

I was surprised to see it was almost 9:30. After a rough start, I had finally fallen into a restless sleep around four in the morning. I had roused less than half an hour ago, still exhausted.

Adam took in my un-brushed hair pulled back into a haphazard bun and baggy t-shirt over yoga pants, and without waiting for a response, lowered himself into the chair beside me.

What had he asked me? Oh yeah, if he was interrupting me.

"Not at all," I told him, only vaguely wondering why he was back so soon.

I indicated my mug. "Would you like some coffee?"

"I've already had a cup today," he said, making himself comfortable in the chair.

I shrugged, glad I didn't have to get up, and turned back towards the water.

"Quite a view you have here."

I nodded.

He tried again. "You know, I've lived all my life in this town and not once have I woken up to the ocean pounding outside my room."

"You don't have friends or family who live along the beach?" I asked, finding that hard to believe.

"I didn't say that," he teased, "I've just never spent the night at their house."

Shaking my head, I ignored his engaging grin and sipped my hot beverage. It was too early and the caffeine hadn't kicked in.

Adam was quiet for a bit and so I chanced a look in his direction.

Something about the way his dark hair fell over his forehead as he leaned back and his muscular arms relaxed against the armrests of the chair made me nervous. This wasn't the all-business cop I was getting to know.

"How was your night?" Adam asked, the laughter completely removed from his voice.

"Fine," I said, trying to ignore the unexpected awareness I was beginning to feel in his presence.

He tilted his head towards me. "You didn't sleep much, I'm guessing."

Mental imprints of the message written on my bathroom mirror had haunted me into the wee hours of the morning. Even though everything was cleaned up by the time I went to bed, my room still felt violated and it had taken hours to calm the anxiety racing through me.

Shaking my head at him and not wanting to divulge how scared I had been, I returned to my mug of coffee. I wasn't sure why he was showing so much concern all of a sudden but it was making me uncomfortable.

"Did you need to ask me more questions?" I asked, trying to direct the conversation to his reason for being here.

"Nope," he replied, closing his eyes and stretching his long legs out in front of him, just like he had the day before while we sat on the porch.

In direct contrast to my nervousness, he looked entirely too comfortable.

"Just checking on you. Making sure you're okay."

I looked over at him uncertainly, not sure what he meant by that. Was he checking on me as a victim, as a suspect or as a person?

"Well, I think I'm fine. Everything always looks better in the morning."

"That it does," he agreed, cracking his eyes open in time to catch me staring at him. I blushed and lifted my gaze to the surf crashing in.

We were silent a moment and I watched the tiny sandpipers running in the wake of the waves along the shore. They were quick to fly as the water spread across the sand in their direction. I felt their nervousness. I wanted to take off too.

"Do you need anything?" His voice was unconcerned, almost lazy. "I'm going to head into the precinct. I could bring back stuff from town, if you need it, when I drive past on my way home."

Now it made sense, I thought with some relief. I was just a stop on his way to town.

"Are you sure you should be helping me?" I inquired, narrowing my eyes at him. "I'm still a suspect. Well, maybe not for murder, but you can't completely write me off for the embezzlement."

He must have found my self-accusation amusing because he laughed.

"All the more reason to keep a close eye on you," he answered, and I turned in time to catch his wink.

His wink stirred something within me and for the first time I had an inkling that Adam might be interested in me as more than just a suspect. Honestly, that idea scared me more than having a possible murderer search my bedroom.

He didn't say anything more and after awhile, as the coffee began to kick in and my heartbeat settled back to normal, I broke the mood with a serious question.

After concluding that Declan's murder was tied up in the embezzlement, there were things I wanted to know.

"Adam, I haven't really learned much about Declan's charges," I began. "I wish I could ask Mr. Talcos but I feel uncomfortable bringing it up."

I blushed as I made the following admission, "I tried looking it up online on my phone but the news reports are vague. Is there anything you can tell me about it?"

Adam tilted his head and met my eye warily.

"Are you sure you want to know? You believe in him now. Wouldn't you like to leave it at that?"

I bit my lip, wondering if he was right. Did I want to know?

I took a deep breath.

"Regardless," I answered, "I think I need to know the truth."

It wasn't a pretty story. Adam had apparently researched it quite a bit because he seemed to know all the gritty details. The story began six years ago when Declan had taken over the research firm. He had been working in the main hub in Boston as a second tier manager before his promotion to CEO. Almost immediately he'd taken over the international component of the company and managed to expand it to five other countries within the first two years.

In addition to enlarging the exportation of the company's research products, he also managed to contract with the US government, garnering funding for research into the Zika virus. Stocks had immediately soared and within weeks the value of the company had increased exponentially.

Through it all Declan had remained focused on the company's values and purpose. Based on the motto *"Non sibi sed omnibus"* or "Not for myself but for all," the company had grown without cutting corners or compromising on ethical decisions.

When his finance board announced a significant discrepancy only six weeks ago, Declan had been the loudest and most verbal supporter of an internal investigation. Once the discrepancy had been substantiated he'd been the one to contact the FBI and ask for their intervention.

Things had taken a strange turn only a matter of weeks later when Declan had suddenly disappeared. The FBI had uncovered proof that only a top-level corporate officer could have so successfully lifted three billion dollars in such a short amount of time.

Declan's untimely departure had done more to make him appear guilty than anything else. As if to put icing on the cake, his secretary had come forward with the information that Declan had asked her to book him a ticket to South America at the last minute and then told her he would be gone for an extended period of time. Rather than abet her employer, she had called the police. Apparently, that had been the night Declan disappeared.

Looking at Adam's face as he recounted the details of Declan's last few days in Boston, I sensed he didn't enjoy sharing any of this with me. It was as if he was sorry he had to tell me things so condemning about the man I'd married.

After he finished his narrative, I sat in disbelief. Things were so much worse than I had originally thought. Declan asking his secretary to book him a ticket, hiding after being accused; those were the actions of a guilty man.

Shaking my head as if to clear it, I clenched my hands, my fingernails digging into my palm and asked, "Do you know what the FBI found? Do they have proof that he was involved? Maybe it was all a misunderstanding and Declan left for a completely different reason?"

I knew I was grasping at straws but I couldn't wrap my mind around the idea that Declan was an embezzler. That wasn't the man I had known.

Adam's deep voice grounded me, "I'm sorry, Aimee. I don't know specifically what they found but it was enough to make Declan run. "

I rose, suddenly unable to sit still. I paced to one end of the deck and back. Adam remained in his chair watching me so after a few more turns I stopped and leaned back against the rail, facing him.

"Thank you for telling me this, but I know Declan didn't steal that money."

A gust of wind blew my messy bun loose and long auburn strands gently fell into my face. I reached behind my back, trying to find my hair tie before giving up and gently tucking the flyaway strands back behind my ears.

Adam's eyes were dark and compassionate as he watched me wrestle, both internally and externally. It was as if he sensed the difficulty I had reconciling this information with the man I had known.

"I think I'd like to be alone right now," I finally said, unable to come up with a better defense of my now-deceased husband.

I licked my lips and could taste salt. Adam stood and looked down at me.

"I'm sorry, Aimee," was all he said.

I shook my head, suddenly pleading, "It's not conclusive evidence," I told him, "only circumstantial."

He frowned and I could tell he was tempted to say more, maybe even something that he wasn't at liberty to share. Instead he awkwardly patted my shoulder, promising to check on me later.

Then he was gone. And I was alone.

I turned back to face the ocean and felt my hair tie come completely undone and fall unheeded. I gripped the rail trying not to believe what Adam had told me. It wasn't Declan. It couldn't have been Declan.

My thought process wasn't rational but the more I contemplated the information I'd been given, the more convinced I became that Adam didn't have the whole story.

The Declan I knew wouldn't rob his own company. For crying out loud, he wouldn't drive away from a gas station without paying for gas. He had also insisted on tipping the housecleaner at the cheap hotels where we stayed, even though the rooms had been remarkably less than clean. A man who had lifted three billion dollars for his own pocket wouldn't care about the living wage of a housekeeper, would he?

Then I remembered the day I woke up with a migraine. I had remained in the car with a splitting headache while Declan ran into a drugstore to pick up some medicine for me. Normally I made the public appearances, paid for gas, bought food, and requested hotel rooms so he was less likely to be noticed. That day he had put me first, risking being seen, in order to take care of me.

I relaxed my white knuckled grip on the rail, flexing my taut fingers. I knew what self-centered men were like. I had seen enough of them while living with my aunt. If Declan was anything, he was considerate. Were considerate men embezzlers?

Perhaps, but once again I felt in my heart that Declan was innocent. Now it was becoming clear, though, that I might be the only one who believed in him. It was time to do something about it.

**Chapter 10**

I needed to talk to more people; the people involved with his company. There had to be something the police and FBI were missing, because they weren't looking for it and because they thought Declan was guilty.

I decided to shower first and get ready for the day. Heading up the stairs, I thought of the few people I knew in relation to Declan. There was his grandfather, of course. And his best friend Eric and his ex-girlfriend Alyssa. I was kind of bumbling in the dark but it was a place to start.

Later as I emerged from my room, I spotted Mr. Talcos coming determinedly down the hall.

"Good morning, Aimee," he said, not waiting for me to return the greeting. "I have a friend coming over in an hour or so, a former business partner. His name is Howard Angle. I'd like to introduce you, if that's okay?"

Since this was the first time Mr. Talcos had asked anything of me, I felt like it was incumbent on me to agree.

"Certainly. Should I start a pot of coffee?"

A delighted smile crossed his face. "Excellent idea. Thank you."

I headed down to the kitchen and got out the beans. Mr. Talcos had a fancy machine in his kitchen that included a grinder. I looked around while the loud whirring grated on my ears. As the grinds filled the cup I glanced over toward the pantry. Maybe I could throw together a small coffee cake.

I started pulling out the ingredients I needed from the shelves, happy to find everything at hand and also grateful for the opportunity to keep myself occupied.

Almost an hour later, Mr. Talcos entered the kitchen, sniffing with gusto. I had just pulled the coffee cake out and its aroma must have permeated to whatever room he'd been waiting in for his friend.

"Aimee," he said, stepping over to inspect the steaming pan, "this looks delicious."

He inhaled and then turned, unexpectedly changing the subject. "I've been wondering about your family. I assume you've been in contact with them, but I want you to know you are welcome to invite them or maybe a friend to come stay with you while you're here. I can't imagine any of this is easy for you."

I was surprised and pleased by the thoughtful gesture. I just wished I knew how to respond. I didn't have any family or friends to send for. Except for two special-needs brothers, the only people I was still in contact with were my two roommates.

The girls hadn't heard from me since the day I disappeared with Declan. They both were under the impression I was on vacation and my brothers had limited understanding. They only knew it had been awhile since I'd visited. The last thing I wanted to do was pull any of them into my present situation.

"I'm okay," I said, a false heartiness in my voice, "I'm sure this will all be over very soon."

Mr. Talcos' response was less reassuring, "I'm not sure things will clear up in the next couple days. Are you sure you don't want to invite someone to stay?"

Thankfully I was saved from explaining the lack of concerned friends and relatives in my life by the ringing of the doorbell.

Mr. Talcos went to answer it and I started pouring out coffee. I could hear muffled voices gradually approaching as Mr. Talcos reentered with an older gentleman in tow.

His friend filled up the kitchen, his broad shoulders and protruding stomach taking up more than twice as much space as Declan's grandfather. Upon closer inspection, I realized he was probably close to the same age as Mr. Talcos but his large girth and hearty tone gave him the appearance of a younger man.

"So this is Mrs. Talcos," he boomed, stepping over to greet me. Expecting a handshake, I was shocked to find myself buried in a hug. Placing me back on my feet, Howard Angle looked down at me from his great height with a sympathetic smile.

"I'm so sorry, m'dear. Don't know quite what else to say. Declan was like a grandson to me. I'm so sorry for your loss and all that. I would have come to the funeral but no one informed me about it until it was over."

I caught the challenging look he sent Mr. Talcos as he let me go.

Taking another step backwards, I murmured a polite thank you. His overwhelming personality was a little off-putting.

Not responding to the implication that he had left Mr. Angle out of the loop, Mr. Talcos introduced his friend to me, this time more formally.

"Aimee, may I present to you Howard Angle? He was my right hand man at Autem Viris. He's retired now but he still spends a lot of time at the office."

The two men couldn't be more different and the contrast was almost humorous. It was hard to picture the two of them at the helm of anything, let alone a very successful company.

I acknowledged the introduction and then sent them out on the back porch with their coffee. Like little boys, they left only after I promised to bring them their dessert.

Several minutes later, I carried out forks and two large slices of still warm cake. The men had moved the chairs closer to the house and sat, conversing intently. I approached quietly, not wanting to disturb them.

As I drew near, I caught the tail end of their conversation, just barely, over the sound of the rolling waves.

Mr. Angle's booming voice carried easily.

"I've spoken with Erik and I've spoken with Nick. Neither one will tell me what's going on with the investigation. They say the FBI is still looking into it and they can't say anything."

Mr. Talcos murmured a reply I didn't quite catch.

"Why did he come here? What was he looking for?" Howard Angle's voice rose higher.

I cleared my throat noisily before Mr. Talcos had a chance to answer and set the tray down on the table between them.

"Enjoy," I said sweetly, stepping back. "I'll be in the house if you need anything."

The two gentlemen thanked me profusely and politely invited me to join them.

After declining, I escaped to the kitchen. Washing up the counters, I thought about what Howard Angle had said. Erik might be the man who had shown up at the funeral, the man whom Mr. Talcos declared was Declan's best friend. But who was Nick? Another CEO at the company? Regardless, I now had another name of someone who might be able to give me more information about the embezzlement.

Impulsively I decided to ask Adam about the two men. I still had his number programmed into my phone from the other day, so after scrolling through recent calls, I sent a quick text message asking him to stop by again tonight. I figured I was more likely to get answers in a face-to-face interview.

I didn't want to say too much but I guess I erred on the side of saying too little because he responded immediately, asking if everything was all right. Smiling at his concern, I texted a short reply, assuring him all was well and I just had some things to discuss.

As I pushed send, I heard the doorbell ring for the second time that day. Assuming the men outside were too far away to hear, I pocketed my phone and went to answer it.

Hesitating once I actually got to the door, I peeked through the window, surprised to see the beautiful woman from the funeral standing on our front stoop. I quickly opened the door and was hit by a radiant smile. Introducing herself as Alyssa, she asked if she could come in.

"I really just wanted to come over and see that you're all right," she said frankly, stepping into the house and looking me over. Her beautiful violet eyes were sympathetic and I realized, with her model-like height, she towered over me.

Stepping aside, I made space for her to completely enter, and closed the door behind her.

"That's very kind of you," I said, unsure how to respond to her effusiveness.

She moved into the hall, ignored my reluctance, and gave me a large hug. I hesitantly returned it.

"I knew Declan most of my life. He was like a brother to me," she said as she let me go.

Her lovely eyes filled with tears. "I want you to know that I know he wasn't guilty of the embezzlement."

Her unsolicited support surprised me and at the same time I felt a rush of relief. Finally, I had met someone who didn't believe Declan was an embezzler.

Feeling like I had finally found an ally, I was overwhelmed with the urge to talk to her. Except, I didn't want to share anything that might be overheard by Mr. Talcos and his friend.

"Would you like to step out for a coffee?" I asked, ignoring the smell wafting from the kitchen. "I'd love to talk with you and quite honestly, I'd like a chance to get out of the house for a bit."

Alyssa seemed happy with this suggestion and offered to drive me in her car. Remembering Adam's admonition not to go out without informing him, I sent him another quick text, this time to let him know I was getting coffee in town with a friend.

As I had only lived here less than a week and had only been out of the house for the funeral, we had to use an app on Alyssa's phone to find a local café.

As we drove, she explained to me she was from Boston, where she'd grown up. Both she and Declan had gone to the same high school and he had been one year ahead of her. She and her husband Erik both worked for the same company, Declan's bioresearch firm. Her declaration that they had worked there 'for ages' made me smile as she didn't seem old enough to have worked anywhere very long.

"What do you do there?" I asked as I held her phone with the navigation system programmed in. She made a turn toward town.

"I'm a researcher in the lab. Erik has a masters in business and is a second tier manager. We met when we both started working for Declan's grandfather about ten years ago. I dated Declan before I dated Erik."

She glanced sideways at me as if to gauge my reaction.

"I heard about that," I told her, trying to reassure her that she wasn't telling me anything new. "I asked Mr. Talcos who you were after the funeral and he said you and Declan dated in high school and briefly after college."

"Yes, it was right before Declan's sister died. Things didn't work out but it was all very amicable. A lot of people think I left Declan to date Erik but the truth is Declan broke up with me. He changed a lot after Elyse's death. I didn't start seeing Erik, I mean dating him, until almost a year later."

I wondered why she was telling me something so personal but then realized she wanted me to know everything about her relationship with Declan. I appreciated the openness and tried to reciprocate.

"What do you know about our marriage?" I asked, opening the can of proverbial worms.

"Not much," she said dryly. "I never heard of you until the funeral when Erik told me who you were. He found out from the undertaker."

I almost smiled but the situation was too serious.

By this time we were in the downtown area of the tiny beach town and had found a cute, colorful little café. Alyssa concentrated on parallel parking before turning the engine off and turning to look at me.

I met her eyes directly. "I met Declan a little over three weeks ago today. He was hiding out and I decided to help him escape. It was a spontaneous decision but I don't regret it."

Her face was comical. "You only knew him three weeks? And you married him? While he was running from the law?"

I shook my head, almost smiling at her shocked tone. "Let's go inside and I'll tell you the whole story."

## Chapter 11

Later, as I sipped a caramel latte and Alyssa dipped a teabag in and out of her hot water, I told her what had happened. I was getting pretty good at it as this was the third time I'd recounted my life with Declan in the past week.

As short as our history was, it surprised me how each time I told the story a new detail would surface. This time as I recounted the particulars, I remembered the night before we arrived at the house. We had stopped at a campground in upstate New York, pulling in after dark. I had gone into the little camp office and paid for the use of a campsite for the night. Assuming we would just sleep in the car, I had started to recline my seat when Declan had reached over and touched my arm.

"How about a campfire? I saw some wood by the office. We could warm up a little and enjoy our last night."

I had studied his face in the half-light reflected from the dashboard. He had looked at me hopefully, almost boyishly and as much as I just wanted to fall asleep, I had given in. As Declan went to reconnoiter for wood, I stepped over to a neighboring campsite and borrowed some matches. Using wrappers from our lunch and dinner as kindling, Declan soon had a large flame going.

We sat up until past midnight, watching as the fire died down and the wood slowly dwindled to embers. The sky had filled with stars and somehow I had found myself leaning against Declan, his arm platonically wrapped around my shoulders. As we fell asleep, I remember thinking that I was exactly where I wanted to be.

Alyssa cleared her throat and I realized I had stopped talking. Aware that I had zoned out, I tried to cover for my mental lapse by checking the messages on my phone. A brief one from Adam acknowledging my text message lit up the screen. I looked back across the table in time to see Alyssa regarding me intently.

The intensity of her gaze caught my attention and I watched her pull a brightly colored purse up and place it on the table in front of us. She unzipped the front pocket and slowly reached inside, her gaze unwavering as she withdrew a black object. Recognizing it as a smart phone, I watched uneasily as she laid it in the space between us.

I sat for a moment, not touching it, not sure why she had brought it out.

"I wasn't sure what to do with this," she began, indicating the phone. "Declan left it behind with Erik when he disappeared and the FBI never asked for it. We thought about turning it over to the police but since no one ever asked for it..."

She finished her sentence with a shrug, as if that were reason enough.

"This is Declan's cellphone?" I clarified.

She nodded.

Hesitating to touch it, I murmured, "He had a burner phone when they searched the house after his death."

"They probably assumed he destroyed this one," she said, her tone matter of fact.

Eyeing it carefully, I reached out and slowly picked it up. Covered with a leather case, I had to release the snap on the front to open it. Then I touched the round button at the base, the screen lighting up instantly.

"It's on airplane mode," Alyssa told me, "so no one can track it."

I frowned and looked up.

"It needs a passcode," I told her.

She responded by cocking an eyebrow at me.

"Any idea what the code could be?" I asked, feeling foolish for no reason, as she now knew how tenuous and short-lived our marriage had been.

She reached over and quickly tapped in four numbers. The lock screen disappeared.

"The last four digits of his social security number," she said, shrugging. "It was his standard numeric password, even back in high school."

The lock screen showed an impersonal star-filled sky, but once open, I saw a sailboat tied to a dock with Declan standing at the helm.

"That was his boat," Alyssa explained, pointing at the picture. "He has more pictures of it in his photo album."

I tapped on the app and immediately it opened to an eclectic group of selfies, friends' faces and beautiful landscapes. I scrolled through a few but felt like I was prying. I turned the phone off and looked up at Alyssa. She had been watching me, her lips pursed. I couldn't tell what she was thinking.

"Why are you giving me this?" I asked confused.

Her face relaxed and she smiled at me in a friendly manner. "Honestly? I'm not completely sure. I guess I thought maybe something in there might help you."

"Help me?" Caution washed over me. I wasn't sure what she was suggesting.

"Well, you are going to find out what really happened, aren't you?" Her gaze challenged me with its directness. I swallowed, unsure what she was insinuating.

Almost to the point of rudeness, I asked her, "What are you asking me to do?"

Her expression didn't change, but she did lean towards me over the little table, saying in a low, urgent voice, "Aimee, I have listened to everything you've told me. I wasn't even sure I was going to give you that phone when I first came here. But after talking to you, seeing how deeply you felt for him, I'm confident that it's the right thing to do. What you do with it?" She sat back in her seat and her voice went back to normal, "Well, that's up to you."

I looked at her for a moment, measuring her words. Her confidence in my ability to do anything recalled me to the resolution I had made just that morning.

"I do want to clear his name," I began, my voice husky.

I cleared my throat. "And I'm willing to do whatever I need to, in order to get to the bottom of this."

A huge smile spread across Alyssa's face and she gave a little whoop.

"But," I tried to caution her, "please don't get your hopes up. It's unlikely I'll find anything."

"I knew I could count on you!" she said, ignoring my disclaimer and smiling at me with approval.

A small flame of excitement caught spark inside me. Despite my fears, my anxiety, and my cautious feelings, I wanted to do this. Declan might be dead, but I still wanted to help him.

"I promised Erik I wouldn't do anything dangerous," Alyssa said, "but I'll do whatever I can to help you that's not especially dangerous."

I laughed at her eagerness. It was so lovely to have a friend.

"Oh!" she gave a little squeal, excitement catching up to her. She reached out to squeeze my hand. "I can tell that you're just as confident as I am that Declan was innocent. Even Erik has trouble believing him."

There were actual tears in her eyes. "I'm certain that if anyone can clear his name, it's you."

Her vehemence overwhelmed me and I asked without thinking, "Why me?"

She drew back, adjusting her purse, "Because you loved him, of course."

Her last few words stalled my elation and inwardly I cringed at her statement. Despite my protestations that ours was a marriage of convenience, Alyssa seemed to believe the same as Mr. Talcos.

"Not love, exactly," I stammered weakly, "I didn't know him well enough to love him."

Had I loved Declan? I was still figuring that out. Putting the whole L-O-V-E word aside, I recognized that a mutual bond of trust had developed between us. I respected him and, what is more, believed him.

"So what are you going to do first?" Alyssa's chipper voice broke into my swirling thoughts. She had finished her tea and wiped up the table with a napkin. Now she sat waiting expectantly, apparently hoping I would come out with a comprehensive plan for proving Declan's innocence.

For a moment I regarded her, my mind churning as ideas came together. Maybe I did have a plan.

"My first step should probably be to go through anything and everything of Declan's that hasn't already been taken by the police. Someone was looking for something in our rooms. Maybe they haven't found it yet."

Which meant maybe I could find it first.

"I also need more information about the embezzlement. Do you think Erik would be willing to talk with me? He's management, right?"

Alyssa nodded enthusiastically. "Of course! When do you want to come over?"

Picking up Declan's phone, I put it in my purse and attempted a smile. "I'm not really sure. I feel overwhelmed by everything. I guess I'll start with going through Declan's phone and the house. Once I'm free to leave town, I can come down to see you."

Alyssa looked confused, "Free to leave town?"

"Yes," I explained, "until the police give me the okay, I'm supposed to stay in the house for my own protection."

"You came here with me," she pointed out.

I nodded, "After letting the detective know and technically I'm still in town."

Her eyes darted around the café, "Do you think they're here, listening in on our conversation?"

I shrugged, amused by her old-world spy dialogue. "Maybe, maybe not. Either way, it's for our own safety."

She stood up, "Well, I'll help you any way I can! Well, I mean, as long as it doesn't endanger us. I promised Erik that."

The slight shrug of her shoulders told me that her definition and Erik's definition of danger might not mesh exactly.

She reached across the table and took my cup.

"Maybe I can talk Erik into coming up here to talk to you," she said.

I laughed and reached out to take it back. "Here, I've got that. And I can call you about getting together after I've gone through the phone and snooped around the house some more."

Placing my empty mug on the counter, I met Alyssa at the door. She looked pleased and held her hand out to me. I thought she wanted me to shake it so I was surprised when she pulled me into a tight hug.

"Thank you, Aimee," she said, "for being so understanding and so good for Declan. He was lucky to find you."

Then she added something that made me blush.

"Regardless of how you felt, I know you meant something to him. He never would have married you otherwise."

Wanting to refute that I was ever anything remotely important to Declan, I found myself speechless. Blatantly denying he cared for me, especially to someone who knew him like a brother, was pointless and arguing that I didn't care for him that way would only embarrass me more.

Pushing the glass door open, I headed to the car. I could hear Alyssa's tinkling laugh as she followed me from behind.

## Chapter 12

When we returned to the house, all was quiet. Howard Angle's black SUV, which I had noticed parked in front of the house when we left, was no longer visible. My car, which Declan and I had driven all the way from Memphis, was still parked around to the side.

Before leaving, Alyssa programmed my telephone number into her contacts and sent me a text to make sure I had her number. Giving me a warm, sisterly hug, she'd asked me to call for any reason and then took off.

I climbed the front steps slowly and then knocked lightly before opening the door, grateful to find it unlocked.

*If I'm planning to leave the house again I should probably ask Mr. Talcos for a key,* I thought to myself.

Going directly to my bedroom, I entered apprehensively, memories of my room in shambles vividly playing in my imagination. All was as it should be and I breathed a small prayer of thanks. I closed the door and locked it, happily avoiding Mr. Talcos for the time being. It was time to look through Declan's phone and for this I wanted privacy.

I turned from locking the door to survey my room. Across from me, the large window was blocked by heavy curtains. I walked over and pushed them aside, letting bright sunlight stream in.

Then I stood there for a moment, watching the ebb and flow of the ocean. Doubting thoughts intruded and I wondered if I should call Adam and have him come get the phone immediately.

Biting my lip, I decided he couldn't fault me too much if I gave it to him the same day I acquired it. That meant I had until this evening to look through it.

My mind made up, I walked over and pulled my pillow from beneath the blue flowered quilt that lay on top of the bed. I put it up against the headboard and then sat down. Flopping backwards, one leg still falling off the bed, I made myself comfortable and reached for my purse strapped over my shoulder.

I hesitated again, this time wondering if Declan would approve of me looking at his phone. Taking a deep breath, I unzipped the top and pulled it out. Then I sat for a moment just holding it in my hands.

This was a connection to a Declan I hadn't known. He wasn't a successful entrepreneur when we were together. He wasn't an intellectual achiever or a superbly wealthy international business owner. He was just Declan, a guy on the run who needed help; a guy whose sweet and generous nature had led me to trust him. In hindsight, though, I had known nothing about him.

Holding up the phone, I took a deep breath and turned it on. A low-level red bar flashed its angry light at me.

Moaning, I sat back up and searched for my own cable. His phone was a newer edition of the one I currently had and I had a miniscule hope that the charger plug might be the same.

Sighing in relief, I fitted my cable to his cell. After connecting it to the electrical outlet beside my bed, I reclined again, this time somewhat forced to stay on my left side as the cord only reached about a foot.

I started by tapping in the passcode from Alyssa and scrolling through his applications. I thought about going to the photos section first but after the quick glance I'd made in the café, I was almost afraid of what I would find there. Photos seemed extremely personal.

For the first time I felt nervous knowing about Declan's private life. What if there was someone special in his past? Some female he had failed to mention to me? Would I be obligated to seek her out and explain?

Scared of finding a picture of Declan with another woman, I quickly opened up his recent text messages. Nothing of interest jumped out as I read through each and every one. Some of the texts between him and Erik actually had me laughing as I scrolled down, realizing that the two shared a unique sense of humor.

I was also surprised to see that he texted his grandfather, or rather Mr. Talcos texted him. I read through them, seeing more than once the directive "call me." Texting was obviously not their primary way of communication.

Reading Declan's texts was like hearing him talk. For a moment I felt a crowding sadness as I remembered that I would never see Declan again, never hear him laugh or joke, or have the opportunity to see if the bond between us could grow into something more.

Sniffling, I quickly perused other, less personal messages, mostly involving work. He appeared to have texted with someone named Nick Santos often. I wondered if he was the same Nick whom Howard Angle had mentioned. I wished I had remembered to ask Alyssa if she knew of anyone by that name.

Finishing all the texts, I backed out of the messages application and found the email icon. As my finger hovered over it, my eyes strayed to the bottom corner where there was a calendar app. Changing my mind, I opened the calendar, swiping the screen back in time until I arrived to the day before Declan had originally disappeared.

I was surprised to see he had five meetings scheduled that day. It seemed like a lot. The first was simply labeled "Monthly Meeting" and I assumed that was a general company meeting. The second followed immediately afterwards and appeared to be with a research group labeled, "Team Spacci." Then there was "Lunch with Erik" at one-thirty followed by two meetings back to back, the first with Nick Santos and scheduled for three-thirty and the second with Howard Angle, which oddly began at five.

I looked over Declan's schedule again. Was it strange that he had meetings with all these people on the day he disappeared? Could that be significant?

I scrolled through, looking for other appointments and realized that Declan had been a busy guy. He averaged two to three meetings a day, many of them teleconferences. I wondered how he had gotten any work done.

Looking closer at the day he disappeared, I noticed a red star beside Howard's appointment. Touching the symbol, a note emerged that said, "Conference call with grandpa."

*How interesting*, I mused, *not just a meeting with Howard, but also with his grandfather.*

I skimmed the rest of the calendar but nothing else of interest popped up.

Going through his email was the same. Nothing of importance jumped out at me.

I even tried logging into the application that contained his work share files. I tried multiple passwords, mostly based on his social security number, but I was unsuccessful.

Finally, I returned to the photo album. My finger hovered over the application for a full thirty seconds before I touched it.

With relief, I realized that Declan's phone must not have been very old as there were only two months worth of pictures. Either that or he was one of those unusual people who routinely upload their photos from their phone to their computer and delete afterwards.

The network sharing option was turned off and as I looked through the pictures, I only encountered fun times. A few photos of him at a baseball game with Erik, a couple of Erik and his wife in the back of a boat, and then some of himself dressed up in a tuxedo. I randomly wondered where he was going and whom he had gone with.

A few selfies later, I realized he was at a wedding and his grandfather had been present. A shot of the bridal party showed he had actually been in the wedding. Judging from the table shot that came up next, it was work related. Howard Angle, Erik, Alyssa and his grandfather sat with Declan standing behind them. Another man, dark with a hooked nose, sat to the right of Mr. Angle. He was next to an older looking woman with puffy hair and lots of make-up.

Laying the phone aside, I no longer felt guilty going through it. In fact, I felt grateful that the device had come into my hands. In a sense, I felt I knew Declan better from seeing his pictures and reading his laid-back, friendly conversations.

That evening when Adam stopped by I was waiting for him on the front porch. I had spent the rest of the day searching: first our bedrooms and then the downstairs. I had failed to turn up a single personal item of Declan's. Between the police and the intruder, everything had been thoroughly cleared out.

Adam climbed the front steps and greeted me with a crooked smile. My heart rate unexpectedly kicked up a gear and I internally berated myself for this involuntary reaction.

He seemed pleased to see me and asked how my day had gone. Not wanting to just throw the phone in his face, I briefly recounted meeting Mr. Angle and my coffee date with Alyssa.

"I'm glad you were able to get out," he said, turning a chair to partly face me before lowering himself down into it. He leaned back, stretching out his long legs in what was becoming a classic pose, and placed his arms on the side rests. I noticed he was wearing jeans this time and I wondered just how accurate cop shows were on television. Weren't detectives supposed to dress a little less casually?

"Did you enjoy meeting Alyssa?" he asked, interrupting my tangential thoughts.

"Yes," I replied, glancing from his legs to his face just in time to see the laugh lines around his eyes wrinkle. I realized he had caught me observing him and blushed slightly.

"Do you know her?" I asked, trying to will away my embarrassment.

"Only by name." His eyes still twinkled.

Rushing to distract him, I held up the phone.

"Alyssa brought me something interesting today," I told him, rocking it gently back and forth to draw his attention. "She wasn't sure what to do with it and thought that since I'm the widow, she should give it to me."

Adam immediately sat up and reached toward the phone, all appearance of a man relaxing after work gone.

"Is this Declan's phone?" he asked, surprise in his voice as I handed it to him.

"Yes," I replied, impressed that he had figured it out so quickly. "Apparently he left it with his friends and they didn't know what to do with it."

"They didn't know to turn it into the police?" he asked incredulously.

I gave him a frown. "Not everyone thinks the way cops do. They regarded it as Declan's private property and felt like they were holding onto it for him, at least while they knew he was alive."

Adam nodded absently and I could see his concentration was on the phone as he snapped open the case with his thumb.

"I'll have to get this down to the precinct and see if they can access it. All we've had are his phone records and emails."

He stared at the now brightly lit lock screen. "This might have some valuable information."

I'm sure my frown revealed my displeasure but I didn't like what I was hearing. Adam hadn't come right out and said he was working on Declan's conviction, but from his latest comment he had to be somewhat involved if he knew what information the FBI had. That worried me.

Reaching across, I took the phone back from Adam who was still staring at the lock screen. He didn't try to stop me. A small shiver travelled all the way from my wrist to my shoulder as my arm brushed his. Ignoring the way my heart rate involuntarily spiked from the slight touch, I punched in the key code and handed it back.

"Alyssa knew the password," I explained in answer to the inquiring look he shot me. "I already looked through it."

"What were you looking for?" he asked, thumbing through the photo album. He paused on the group picture I had noticed earlier.

I took a deep breath. It was time to say something.

"I was looking for something to clear Declan's name."

Instead of the confidence I wanted to project, my face flushed and I looked down at my hands.

"He didn't do this and I intend to do everything possible to find out who did."

Adam stopped and examined me for a second before looking back down at the phone. He closed out the photo album and scrolled through the pages of apps. Then pressing the side button firmly, he shut it off.

"Plenty of time to go through this later," he said, snapping the case shut and standing up. He slipped it in his pocket. "Are you up for a walk on the beach?"

His question caught me off guard. It was like I hadn't just announced my intention to track down a murderer.

"Come again?" I said unthinkingly.

He laughed and held out a hand. "Come walk on the beach with me."

I looked at his hand uncertainly and then suddenly realized I wanted to hold it.

I let him pull me to a standing position but then shyly let go almost immediately.

Kicking off my shoes, I preceded him down the front steps. We walked around the side of the house on the small, brick-lined path, through the dunes and then onto the beach.

The sand was cool and fresh between my toes. We walked along, the waves rolling close but not quite touching my feet. Although Adam didn't take my hand again, we walked slowly and quietly enough that I began to feel nervous. The moment felt intimate, clothed in awkward silence.

I wondered if I should start a conversation; maybe reiterate my resolution to clear Declan's name or something. I hadn't expected Adam to just ignore my statement, especially when part of me secretly wanted his help.

At the same time I decided to repeat myself, Adam cleared his throat and began to speak. I listened closely, focusing on the end of the beach, a miniature lighthouse on the horizon.

"Aimee, I'm not sure how to say this."

He tone was hesitant and at the same time it sounded like he was frustrated with me. Warning bells went off in my head.

He cleared his throat again. "Somehow you've managed to land yourself in the middle of a dangerous criminal investigation. And based on the message left on your mirror, you're not flying under the radar."

I glanced up at him. "You're telling me not to pursue this, aren't you?"

He hesitated and I remained silent, trying to figure out what he wasn't saying.

"Three billion dollars isn't a joke," he answered, "I'm worried that someone out there thinks you either have the money or you know where it is. And they want it."

I watched him, trying to discern if he was upset or just concerned, but he continued to stare straight ahead with his poker face, not looking at me.

"That's what you think the message meant?" I asked, probing. It made sense that the person sending the message was somehow tied into the embezzlement but I hadn't gotten as far as figuring out why he was trying to scare me. Maybe Adam had a point.

Adam turned his head, his eyes briefly meeting mine and then flicking away.

"I'm not sure what it means. But it makes sense that someone was searching for something. What else would they think you have besides the money?"

I frowned and tried to follow his line of reasoning. Unfortunately it made sense.

"But I don't!" I said, almost desperately. "Why can't you see this from my perspective? He didn't have the money and I don't have it!"

I took a deep, ragged breath and halted, almost stomping my foot in denial as an epiphany came to me.

"Maybe Declan was trying to prove who was behind all this. He spent all his time at his grandfather's house looking for something on that computer. He wanted to get out of here before his grandfather came home but only if he could find what he was looking for. Declan knew something."

My brain followed this train of thought, frantically trying to justify my claims even though I had nothing more than surmises to go on.

Adam had stopped when I did and now he turned towards me, his expression speculative when I had expected ridicule.

"That's an angle I haven't examined," he said frowning. I had to lean back slightly and look upwards to see his face; we were so close together. I could tell he was contemplating my hastily thrown together hypothesis.

"Regardless," he said pointedly, surprising me by reaching out and gently cupping my elbows, "You don't need to look into this. It's not a game, Aimee."

"I know it's not a game!" I said, pulling my elbows out of his grasp and stepping back. "And I'm already involved!"

Adam leaned towards me, narrowing the space but not touching me. His eyes searched mine.

"You're not going to let this go, no matter what I say," he said with a glare.

I shook my head, tight-lipped.

He sighed. "I need you to promise you'll be careful and run everything and anything that you come across through me. I don't want you alone and I don't want you going off and getting hurt."

My heart soared as I realized two things. One was that Adam didn't believe I was involved in the murder or the embezzlement and the other was that he cared what happened to me. I felt myself drawn towards him as our gazes locked.

"Do you promise?" he asked, his hands coming up to rest on my elbows again.

"Promise what?" I returned breathlessly, my mind blank except for the realization that Adam was pulling me closer to him.

"To run anything you find by me immediately."

I nodded.

Turning into jelly and not being able to think is apparently funny. Adam laughed at my response and the spell was broken. As a flush erupted up my neck and over my face, I stepped away and muttered, "Of course, I promise."

I turned and strode down the shoreline, ignoring his dancing eyes and goofy grin.

"I'm going to figure this out," I called over my shoulder, hoping he couldn't see my reddened, warm skin.

"Figure *what* out?" was his response and the amusement in his voice made me walk faster. He hurried to catch up beside me and I blushed again. Did he think I meant figure out what had just happened between us?

"I mean," I said, ignoring his teasing tone and continuing to march on, "I need to find out who the real embezzler is. Once we know that we can find out who killed Declan."

Adam easily kept up with me and for a few steps I felt his hand brush against mine. I quickly pulled away, awkwardly linking my now tingling fingers together as I continued to stomp down the beach.

A few minutes later he said over my shoulder, in an even tone, "I wish I could convince you to just stay out of this."

"I can't stay out of this," I retorted, still embarrassed and in a hurry to get back to the house.

"Whoever it is," I continued my rapid pace, trying to ignore Adam's persistent nearness, "he thinks I know something or have something. That's why he threatened me. That's why he's here."

## Chapter 13

I slowed as we drew closer to the house.

Adam shook his head, evidently not quite on board with my reasoning. "It's more likely that Declan had a partner and tried to pull a fast one on him or her. It makes sense that his partner now wants access to the funds and he thinks he can get it through you."

"If that were the case," I shot back, "wouldn't the partner be contacting me directly? And why would Declan marry me? Why bring in another person if he already had help?"

I came to a halt. "If he had a partner, he wouldn't need another one."

At this point I was angry and Adam's ability to contradict my theories didn't help.

His tone was mild as he responded, "Because they had a falling out? Because Declan wanted all, not half? I don't know. When he found you, what he really needed was help getting his money out of the country. He probably would have abandoned you as soon as that was accomplished."

I didn't care how reasonable he sounded, the idea of Declan using me made me see red.

"If he needed my help moving it out," I said, raising my voice an octave, "then where is it? Cause I certainly can't move it if I don't have it!"

"Aimee, his death was premature. He probably planned to tell you but died before he had time."

I gulped, trying to calm down.

"If you start with the assumption that Declan is guilty," I finally choked out through gritted teeth, "you'll never look for the real thief. You'll only see what you want to see instead of what really happened. This is why I need to be involved, because every other person investigating this case thinks just the same as you."

Adam's eyes narrowed as he pulled back. "I'm keeping all my options open. I can't dismiss the possibility that Declan might have been involved, because the woman who loved him," his voice grew louder, "thinks he didn't do it."

I looked at him in disbelief, my anger temporarily suspended. "You think I'm defending him because I loved him? You don't know anything."

I turned to walk away but Adam grabbed my arm, detaining me. I looked at his hand and then up at him.

He licked his lips uncomfortably. "Aimee, I know feelings cloud judgment. And I know you felt strongly for him. Why else would you defend him so vigorously?"

I thought about this for a moment. Pulling my arm free, I put my hands on my hips and gazed at his chin, unable to look him in the eye. Had I loved Declan?

I raised my eyes. "Regardless of my feelings, which you have no right to make assumptions about, I think you owe Declan the right to a fair trial. Which means you can't make him guilty before you have all the evidence."

This being said, I turned around and trudged up the sand trail to the house.

I heard Adam call my name. He hurried up behind me but I didn't stop.

"Aimee, don't you think if we didn't already have evidence, I wouldn't be so sure?" he called over my shoulder.

I stopped in my tracks, his words freezing my heart.

"All evidence points to a top-level manager at his company as the only one who could pull off the heist. No one could have run those numbers through the computer or withdrawn that much money without tipping someone off right away."

He paused and took a deep breath. "He had to intimately know the inner workings of the company. There are only three people involved at that level and Declan is the only one who tried to run."

His words slammed into me and I wondered why I was hearing this for the first time. I thought of my previous conversations with both him and Mr. Talcos, and the vague explanations I'd received from both of them.

I turned to face him.

"Who are the other two CEOs?" I asked, the name Nick Santos passing through my mind.

Adam didn't answer. I saw the reticence on his face. He didn't want to tell me.

As if on cue he said, "I'm not sure I should say anything more. You're already much more involved than you should be and as I keep saying, I don't want to see you hurt."

I eyed him irritably.

"Don't you think it's a little too late to hold back now? I could go ask Mr. Talcos."

Not that I knew if he would tell me either. I sighed. It didn't signify.

I watched as Adam wrestled with himself before coming to a startling decision. Plopping down in the sand, right in the middle of the pathway that led between the dune grass and up to the house, he motioned for me to sit. Hesitantly, I joined him.

"Declan is understandably the FBI's top suspect since he is the highest ranking and only active CEO.

However his grandfather and his grandfather's former business partner, Howard Angle, both have sufficient experience and access to siphon money like that out of the company. Howard retired last year."

He paused and I could tell he was forming his thoughts, probably debating how much to tell me.

"The question is why. All three men are well off, still own large shares of the company, and have no debts that we are aware of. Their financial records are clean and their personal histories are stellar. Howard Angle has been married to the same woman for over forty years and has six grandchildren. Alfred Talcos retired because he wanted to spend more time on his charitable organizations after his wife of forty-nine years passed away. We've tried following different leads and different possibilities for other high level managers but all roads seem to lead back to Declan. Maybe being a multi-millionaire wasn't enough for him. Maybe he thought he needed billions."

Even as he said it, I could tell Adam didn't believe it. "Regardless of motive, the money was taken. And as the FBI's investigation is revealing, it just wasn't possible to take that much money out in so little time without having Declan's ties and access."

I looked at him speculatively. "Adam, for one minute, pretend you were going to rob a company. How would you go about it? You couldn't just go in under your own name to transfer out billions of dollars. You'd have to go in through the one or two people who actually had access to the bank accounts."

I stopped, waiting to see if he was following me, "Now pretend you're Declan. You find out your company has been embezzled and when you look into it, you realize that it was done under your name and with your authorization. What do you do? Do you go to the FBI and say, I know it looks like me but I'm sure someone was just trying to frame me? Or do you think that maybe you might be able to find the perpetrator because it obviously has to be someone you know. After all, this is your company and they stole the money from it under your name."

Adam was pensive as he listened to me. Tilting my head to the side, I could see him ruminating as he took in what I was saying.

Then he surprised me and reached out for my hand.

"Aimee, I'm not ruling anything out at this point. Yes, that could have happened. And yes, you're right, at this point we don't know the whole story. I'm not going to declare Declan guilty of anything until we know for sure."

I knew he was trying to be reassuring and at the same time I suspected he just wanted to appease me. I also realized that by acknowledging the possibility that Declan was innocent, he had already started to regain my respect.

I stood up, brushing the sand off my pants. The sincerity radiating from his eyes supported his words and for the first time I didn't completely resent his suspicions of Declan's guilt.

I gave him a conciliatory smile. "If we could just locate the money, that might tell us who took it, right? I mean, if someone is hiding three billion dollars, eventually it's gotta show up, don't you think?"

Adam's face lit up in amusement as he rose to his feet.

"Your ability to continually come up with another theory regarding Declan's innocence is rather disconcerting."

His blue eyes darkened as he reached out and took my chin in his hand, barely touching me.

"Aimee, I'm telling you this because I want you to be careful, not because I want you to solve the case."

I nodded, averting my gaze. In order to escape his concern and my embarrassment, I pulled out of his grasp and ran up the sandy path to the back deck.

Only after I entered the house and left Adam behind did I realize that once again I had forgotten to ask about Nick Santos. I didn't go back out. I needed time away from Adam.

As I set the table for dinner that same evening, I thought about asking Mr. Talcos about Nick. Although I hesitated to bring up Declan or anything related to the investigation, I thought maybe it was safe to inquire after a possible friend.

I had thrown together a simple pasta dish and salad. I really didn't have much energy after searching the entire house that afternoon, and then there was the crazy, confusing walk I'd taken on the beach with Adam.

Mr. Talcos joined me at the kitchen table just as I set the glasses of iced tea in front of each place setting.

"It smells delicious," he said, greeting me with a kiss on the cheek.

"How are you doing?" I asked, measuring his color and energy level. Both seemed improved.

He assured me he was fine and inquired after my well-being. His concern was touching and I thought again how alike he and Declan were.

Serving the food up into dishes, I joined him at the table. I noticed he paused for just a moment with his head bowed before beginning to eat. I said nothing and started in on my own plate.

We chewed in silence before my grandfather-in-law began filling the emptiness with small talk.

As we sat back afterwards, sipping our tea, I turned the conversation to the one name that had been flitting around my head all day.

"Mr. Talcos," I began in my typically blunt fashion, "When Mr. Angle was here I heard him mention the name Nick. Is that the same Nick that Declan worked with, Nick Santos?"

Mr. Talcos looked surprised at the question but after wiping his mouth with a napkin he readily answered.

"Yes, it is. Nick is a family friend. He works independently for Autem as a contractor. He has for over a decade. Oh, and he was once engaged to Elyse, Declan's sister, but they broke up before she died."

I wanted to ask why but didn't want to pry into Elyse's life, remembering how emotional he became when he spoke about her last time.

"Did you meet with Declan the day he disappeared?" I asked, changing the subject. I was thinking of the calendar and the conference call listed that afternoon between him, Declan and Howard Angle.

He looked at me curiously. "No, why are you asking?"

I squirmed before answering. "Umm, I found out from Alyssa who was on Declan's appointment list the day he left. Nick was one of them, you were another."

Technically that was true. She had given me the phone where I'd found the schedule.

"Interesting," he said, looking down at his food again.

"So," I asked, "what does Nick do exactly?"

Mr. Talcos looked up. "He's a programmer. He develops and maintains the system that records and balances company transactions as well as the program that stores our research findings. Honestly, he's somewhat of a genius. Whatever we need, he creates."

"Sounds invaluable," I commented.

"The FBI has him going through the records so they can access information easily."

I eyed him. "He can access the company's financial records?"

"He can view them," Mr. Talcos explained, "but he can't change them."

I chewed on that information for a moment.

"Was he invited to the funeral?"

Mr. Talcos hesitated but answered, "Yes but he was unable to come with all that was going on at the company."

I frowned. Erik and Alyssa had found time to come and they worked at the same place. That led me to another thought.

"Why didn't you invite Mr. Angle?"

He shrugged. "An oversight."

I eyed him as his focus returned to his empty plate, aware that he had nothing more to say. Not even a minute later he pushed away from the table and stood up.

"Thank you, Aimee, for a delicious meal. I can clean up."

I refused his help and he left the room. I sat alone, wondering again about Declan's last day at work. What had he talked about with Nick? What had he talked about with Erik? What had he talked about with Howard Angle?

Time to find out.

## Chapter 14

After cleaning up supper I stepped through the sliding glass doors and out onto the back deck. It wasn't quite dusk yet but the sun was close to setting. Shadows darkened around me and I shivered, looking out at the ocean and realizing someone could be watching me, even now.

What if Adam was right and someone thought I had the money? Three billion dollars was a decent motivation for anyone to seek me out or threaten me.

*Odd that Adam had felt the need to say anything in the first place*, I mused as I walked up to the rail.

His initial warning when we started our walk came back to me. His concern had seemed almost ludicrous in the bright light of day but took on an almost frightening certitude as I stood by myself on the back porch, the cool evening wind raising goose bumps on my arms.

I felt anger rekindling as I thought of his assumptions about Declan. Then the memory of being pulled towards Adam came unbidden and I blushed, remembering how my mind had gone completely blank as he asked me to promise to be careful.

I looked out at the darkening sky, the sea grey as the sun began to set. Adam was right, I did need to be on guard, but not for the reasons he thought. It disturbed me but I couldn't deny that his concern made me feel protected.

In order to distract myself, I pulled my phone from my pocket and sent a text to Alyssa, thanking her for meeting me for coffee earlier. I also let her know I had searched the phone and the house without discovering anything. I didn't think Declan's schedule of meetings counted. I wasn't even sure why they seemed so important except to make me wonder if any of the people he had talked to that day were the catalyst for his departure.

My thoughts returned to Adam's comments about the other top CEOs, albeit retired, having the capability to transfer out the money. I had trouble suspecting Mr. Talcos. For one thing, I knew he loved his grandson. Even while admitting his doubts, he had shown pride in Declan's accomplishments and defended his character. For the other, he had an alibi for the morning of the murder. If I kept to the theory that the same person committed both crimes, then it ruled him out. For a third, it was obvious that he was worried and grieving for his grandson, but nothing made me think he was scared for himself.

Then there was Howard Angle. I obviously didn't know the man well but I was much happier to suspect him than Declan or his grandfather. Plus there was the fact that Declan had an appointment scheduled with him the day he disappeared. Just how close was the relationship between the partners? If they were that tight, then why was Howard Angle not invited to the funeral? Was it truly an oversight?

I pondered why Declan had brought me here in the first place. What was he looking for? Was it because he trusted his grandfather and wanted to see him? But no, Declan had mentioned to me at least twice that he hoped his grandfather wouldn't be here. For the first time I wished I'd asked my husband more questions. I was beginning to think that the only one who knew what had really happened was Declan, and he was gone.

By this point the sun had set and it was almost completely dark. The light on the back porch was motion sensitive and clicked on as I turned back towards the house. I was getting cold, so I re-entered. Remembering that I had left my shoes on the front porch before my walk with Adam, I went to retrieve them.

I made my way to the front door, turning on the outside lights before passing through to the porch. I spotted them sitting beside the chair I'd vacated just hours before and reached down to grab them. Turning and straightening at the same time, I looked up and stopped in my tracks. In thick black letters my name had been spray painted across the white house siding, starting on the right side of the door and getting larger with each letter. A large X was drawn across the center.

I sucked in my breath and then released it again, the shoes dropping heedlessly out of my numb hands. Fighting the urge to panic, I ran inside, slammed the door and locked it. Not even hesitating, I pulled out my phone and with fat fingers found Adam's contact info and called him.

I waited while it rang: once, twice, a third time. Finally, on the fourth ring he picked up and from his voice I could tell he thought this was a social call.

"Aimee?" His voice drifted across lazily. "What's up?"

Uptight, I squeaked out that there was a message spray painted across the front of our house.

He didn't curse but there was a pause where he might have said a few choice words in his head. He immediately became all business and began to question me, wanting more details. I answered, my words tripping over themselves and then listened until I heard his tired sigh.

"It's a shame Mr. Talcos only put a camera on the back porch. I'll be over shortly. Find him and wait with him."

"Adam," I whispered, "what if he's inside?"

Adam's confidence reassured me. "I don't think he'd take the time to graffiti the house if he meant to go inside. Go find Mr. Talcos and lock yourselves into a room.

I ran upstairs, searching for Mr. Talcos after calling for him below. I found him in the small salon that was adjacent to his living quarters. He sat in a recliner, his eyes closed and the bags underneath standing out like a football player's reflection paint.

I stopped and watched him sleep. He had aged ten years since our first encounter only days before.

Suddenly I trembled as a small gust of wind from the window pushed the curtains into the room. I slammed and locked the door, rushing forward to shut the window. I turned toward the startled man now watching me from his rocker. It didn't matter that we were on the second floor, I was not taking chances with the doors or windows.

"Mr. Talcos," I said, probably making him more nervous than was warranted with my breathless, high-pitched squeak, "someone was here. They spray-painted the front of the house."

I must have looked pale because he told me gruffly to sit down before I fainted.

"I called Adam," I told him as I collapsed on a nearby chair.

I regained my composure as I rested back into the soft cushions. Then I took in the pallor of his complexion.

"Are you okay?" I asked, suddenly feeling guilty for springing the information on him so suddenly and dramatically.

He frowned and answered tersely, "I'm fine."

We waited together in silence.

By the time Adam arrived, it was completely dark outside. I saw the headlights turn into the drive and freaked out a little as we waited for the unseen occupants to come up to the house.

A moment later, Adam's number showed up on my caller ID and after ascertaining he was below, I raced downstairs to let him in.

I must have looked as bad as I felt because he pulled me into a brief hug before letting me go. I looked behind him but he was alone.

"How do you always get here so fast?" I asked, trying to regain my composure.

Another set of car lights turned into the driveway.

"I live literally two miles down the road," Adam replied, drawing my attention back to him.

"Did you see…" my voice trailed off.

"I saw," he answered, lightly propelling me further into the house with a hand on my lower back.

We went upstairs and rejoined Mr. Talcos while the other officers came in, checking the porch and scouring the damage.

Less than ten minutes later, Adam went back down and left us waiting in silence. I walked restlessly over to the window where I could see the glow of flashlights slowly working their way through the front yard and around the side of the house. The police were doing their job.

When Adam came back into the room, I could tell he was upset. He tucked his phone down into his pocket and rubbed a hand over his forehead before looking at me.

"I'm not sure what this means," he began. "In addition to the front of the house, there is a message on the side that says, 'Time is running out!' Not original but definitely gets the point across."

Adam's eyes met mine and I knew he was referencing our conversation earlier.

"He's targeting you," he said.

I nodded and bit my lip. Automatically, I slowed my breathing. This was not a time to hyperventilate.

Adam continued, "I think I'd feel better if the two of you moved into a hotel for the next couple of days while we investigate. Somewhere in town with more people nearby and where I can keep a better eye on who comes and goes."

In my heart I knew he was right, but I didn't want to leave. Despite my fears, I wanted to get to the bottom of this and I was pretty sure being holed up in a hotel room wouldn't provide me much opportunity for figuring out who had embezzled from the company or who had killed Declan.

Mr. Talcos inadvertently made the decision for me. Standing up and swaying slightly, he looked even more fragile than he had sitting in the chair.

"Maybe we can pack and leave tomorrow morning, young man. I, for one, need another night in my own bed."

He gestured towards me.

"And I'm pretty sure my grandson's wife would say the same."

Adam acquiesced without hesitation. He apparently saw the same exhaustion on Mr. Talcos' face that I did.

"I'll station an officer in front of the house and one downstairs for the night," he replied, "then we'll get you moved out in the morning."

Adam made a thorough search of the bedrooms before letting us retire. I thought about going back down and checking the doors and windows before heading to bed, but it had been a long day and I trusted Adam to lock up the house.

Plus I remembered, as I finished brushing my teeth, that Adam had said something about a cop spending the night in the house. Although this was reassuring, after two threats personally directed at me, I bolted my door and checked the window lock before climbing into bed. Surprisingly, sleep claimed me almost instantaneously.

The next morning I rolled over to see the digital clock next to my bed blinking an outlandish time. Reaching out for my phone on the bedside table, I checked it and realized it was almost nine o'clock. *We must have lost power during the night*, I thought.

After a quick shower, I dressed and pulled my wet hair back in a clip. Skipping makeup, I made my way downstairs to find a sleepy Adam in the kitchen. I stopped to watch him from the doorway. He was puttering around the coffee pot, looking very much at home.

"What are you doing here?" I asked, entering cautiously and sounding more accusatory than I meant to.

He looked up at my voice and grinned, looking tired but happy to see me.

"I said I would station someone here to keep an eye on you."

His grin widened as I came further into the room. "You were here all night?"

He winked so quickly I almost didn't catch it. "I kept waiting for you to come down. I figured you'd want to talk things over."

"I didn't know it was you," I stuttered and then realized I had made it sound like I would have come down if I'd known he was there. Blushing, I looked over at the coffee pot.

"That stuff ready?" I asked gruffly, trying to change the subject.

"Need a cup?" he asked, mercifully letting my comment go. He walked over and grabbed a mug from the cabinet, filling it without waiting for a response.

"Milk? Sugar?"

"Yes, both."

He doctored the black liquid until it was a creamy brown.

"Mr. Talcos up yet?" I asked, sliding out a stool from the counter and clambering up.

Adam slid the steaming cup in front of me but stayed on the other side of the kitchen bar.

"He was down earlier. I think he's packing. Did you sleep okay? Storm didn't wake you?"

I nodded and sipped my coffee. "Is that why the power went out?" I asked.

He nodded, "There are old and failing power lines along this stretch of road. One of these days the power company will have to replace them but it's an expensive undertaking. Most of the houses along here have generators for emergencies."

"Just not this one," I responded, my mind perking up as caffeine invaded its receptors.

Adam picked up his coffee and took a sip, gazing at me. I became conscious of my makeup-less face and wet hair as he continued to stare and not say anything.

Self-conscious, I asked about growing up in a beach town. That kicked him out of his sleep-deprived reverie and he told me funny stories about tourists who came into his uncle's local surf shop. I was surprised to hear that people surfed in the cold Atlantic water but he assured me that though it wasn't the most popular sport, there was a definite group of dedicated diehards. The surfers who did brave the frigid temps wore wetsuits unless it was the height of summer.

"People mostly came in to buy t-shirts with our logo on them," he explained, downplaying the excitement of interacting with surfers.

I thought about Memphis and what he would think if I told him that I'd never seen the ocean, or a surfer, until I came to Maine with Declan. My parents had talked about a beach trip before they died but we had never gone. Life after my parents' death was self-explanatory.

Then I realized he was laughing and knew that I had missed something.

"What did you ask?" I said, trying to look like I was paying attention.

His dark blue eyes danced. "I asked how you ended up cleaning toilets. It must be an interesting story, you looked deep in thought."

"Oh!" I wondered how long I'd been ignoring his question. "Sorry my mind wandered. And that's not an interesting story."

He chuckled again and relaxed forward on his elbows, folding his palms under his chin before smiling across at me. Once again I was distracted but not by my memories.

Trying to reign myself in, I answered his original question, "Cleaning toilets wasn't my full-time job. I'm a telemarketer and have been for the past six years."

"You're the one who leaves all those automated messages on my phone?"

I gave him a look.

"It paid the bills. I was putting aside money for college. With the stadium job, I finally had enough to start this fall."

Adam tilted his head curiously. "What are you going to study?"

I liked that he talked about it like I would still be going.

"Social work," I answered.

"What made you pick that?"

I looked away. "I just thought it would be nice to help people."

As the second shot of caffeine started to kick in, a thought occurred to me.

"Don't you already know all about me from your police reports?"

Adam had the grace to look sheepish.

"Maybe the big things like where you work," he answered, lifting his chin, "but the little things like why you waited to start college or took a job cleaning toilets? Absolutely not."

He tilted his head to one side and looked at me. "The reasons why you've made the choices you have? I can try to read into it but it would only be a guess."

His searching gaze made me uncomfortable and I wondered if he was referring to my decision to leave my job and follow Declan. I stood up, slipped off the stool and picked my cup up off the counter.

"I'm going to sit outside," I announced, turning and heading out of the kitchen without a backwards glance.

He followed me to the deck where I positioned a chair to face the ocean and sat down. I thought how weird it was that I was sharing a morning cup of coffee with Adam, like it was a normal thing.

"So tell me about your family," he said, settling his mug on his stomach after reclining in one of the chairs next to me.

"What do you want to know?" I asked, knowing there were parts I wasn't keen to share with anyone.

Of course he went straight to those parts.

"I know your parents died when you were young and you have two older brothers who live in a group home. Your aunt was your guardian until you moved out, but you also left before you were eighteen."

I watched him apprehensively, wondering what he thought of a girl who ran away from home.

He continued, obviously sorting through what he remembered from my file. "Your aunt's got a record so I'm surprised they sent you to live with her in the first place."

Rather than condemnation I saw compassion as he recited my history. This made it a little easier to open up and at the same time I wasn't sure how much to tell him. I began hesitantly to explain the logistics.

"I ran away during her first arrest for possession. By the time the courts handed down her slap-on-the-wrist sentence and figured out that she cared for a ward, I had already passed my eighteenth birthday. At that point, they couldn't touch me and quite honestly, I think they were relieved to have one less person on their radar."

I turned away from him, finding it easier to talk without his obvious concern in my line of vision. "I remember the social worker who was assigned to our case coming to visit me in the aftermath. She told me I had a good head on my shoulders and if I wanted to, I could make something of myself."

Memories of that day intruded, and I continued talking, more open with Adam than I'd ever been with anyone about my situation before.

"I believed her. She gave me a list of contacts and with help I earned my diploma by attending night school. I couldn't go during the day because I was sleeping most mornings after working night shift stocking shelves in a grocery store."

I glanced at him. "I lied about my age to get that job."

His expression didn't change and he nodded for me to go on.

"Pretty much all my classmates were pregnant and in many ways much more desperate than I, though I wouldn't have acknowledged that at the time. I was living in a shelter and trying to work enough hours to afford rent somewhere. Eventually after I found the job stocking shelves, two of my classmates invited me to move in with them."

I waited for Adam's reaction. I knew my history was a little off-putting but he remained stoic. He had a cop face, I supposed, and was used to all kinds of crazy narratives. Somehow, though, I didn't want to be just another story to him.

"How was it?" he asked as the silence lengthened between us.

"Completely different from living with my parents or the shelter or even my aunt and her crazy boyfriends, but it was good for me. I learned how to be a friend."

If he thought my response was strange, he didn't say so.

"Were they pregnant?" he asked, continuing the conversation.

"Yes, both of them," I said, grinning at the memories. "I went through not one, but two crazy hormonal teenage women giving birth."

I answered his next question before he could ask, "They both chose adoption."

Those were times that would remain forever branded in my memory. We might not have gone through nights with screaming babies, but I had been present for both of my friends' deliveries. And again in the nights that followed, both of them had broken down and cried, knowing they had done the best thing they could for their children, and at the same time mourning the little lives they would never know. None of that had been easy, for them or me.

"What happened to your friends?" Adam asked, his voice low with sympathy. I blinked back tears, embarrassed to realize I was becoming teary.

"One of them got pregnant again a year later. She moved in with her boyfriend. I haven't seen her since. I still room with my other friend, Amanda, and another friend of hers. Amanda is in her final semester at college. She'll be graduating soon."

"So Amanda was able to go to college?"

Adam's voice was curiously devoid of judgment and I answered a bit cynically.

"Amanda has parents who are willing to help her with her rent and tuition."

Not that I resented Amanda's opportunities, it's just that my life was on a different course. Not having a lot of savings and not knowing if I would even like school were two of the reasons I had decided to put off going until I could actually pay for my first year of school. The third was probably my biggest reason: Fear. I didn't know if I could do it.

"Didn't your parents' death provide you with some money?" Adam's question broke into my reflections.

I looked over at him, surprised he'd ask something so personal. "Most of the money went to supporting my brothers. The small amount the estate left my aunt for my care was quickly spent on drugs."

Adam nodded understandingly and I stared at him, waiting to see censure or some sort of disapproval in his expression. Instead I saw something that reminded me disconcertingly of respect.

Unwilling to talk any more about that period of my life, I switched topics. "Enough about me, how did you end up becoming a detective? Is it what you always wanted to be?"

I took in his clean-cut hair and strong jaw, his wholesome good looks showcasing a healthy, happy childhood. He'd probably grown up an all-American kid with apple pie, baseball and the whole nine yards.

So I was caught off guard when Adam ignored my question and said sincerely, "Can I tell you how much I admire you?"

I shook my head in surprise, not sure I had heard him right. "What do you mean? I've held a minimum wage job, barely paid my rent and done nothing with my life in the past seven years. Do you know what I have to show for that? A bag of clothing and an old car that could die at any moment."

He smiled in return.

Was he mocking me? I tried to read his expression. It was impossible.

I continued, "You're a detective. You probably finished four years of high school, went to prom, got into college, graduated on a scholarship and then worked your way up the police ladder, or whatever they call it."

He stiffened in his chair, turning until he was fully facing me.

"That's just the point," he said, not taking his eyes off mine. "I've spent my whole life furthering my own plans, looking to advance my own career, and worrying how people see me. You could care less about that kind of stuff. If you did, you wouldn't have gone with Declan. You wouldn't have lived with unwed mothers or assisted at their births."

His eyes narrowed. "And you wouldn't be working to prove Declan's innocence right now. I think you need to give yourself more credit. So you didn't go to college. So your aunt's a coke-head. Yet despite all that, you are an amazing person."

I shook my head at him but his admonition struck a chord. It's hard to put into words but up until now I had felt, for want of a better word, like a loser. There was nothing admirable about working two minimum wage jobs while barely paying the rent. Sure I had dreams of college, but I had yet to realize them. Outside of my two roommates, I had no friends. Yes, I visited my brothers and loved them, but they were taken care of by the state. I myself did nothing to contribute to their wellbeing.

The reality, I told myself as I pondered his compliment, was that until Declan walked into my life, I had nothing to show for the twenty-four years I'd been on this earth.

Rather than argue with me, Adam mercifully moved on.

"Your brothers were adopted, weren't they?"

"Yes," I answered, surprised he knew that detail. "My parents thought they couldn't have children so they adopted two boys with Downs Syndrome. I was a surprise."

"Was it difficult?"

"Was what difficult?" I asked, confused.

"Sharing your parents?" he inquired, his question soft and considerate.

"I never thought about it," I mused, pleasant memories clinging to the periphery of my mind. "It was just the way life was. And my parents died so young. I loved them, I loved my brothers, and I always felt loved by all of them in return."

"Do you see them often?" he gently pried and I couldn't tell if he wanted to know because he cared or because he was investigating me.

"My brothers? Until this happened, I used to go every Saturday morning before work to visit. They probably wonder what happened to me."

I hadn't thought of contacting my brothers to let them know I was okay. I wondered if I should call them.

Adam looked at me uncertainly and I liked what he said next. It definitely didn't follow the tenor of an interrogation. "I'd like to go with you someday and meet them."

Smiling shyly in return, I told him I would like that.

"What about you?" I asked, finally turning the tables. "Do you have any siblings? Parents?"

He smiled and took a sip of his coffee before answering.

"I have one brother. He's a big, fancy lawyer in Boston. He comes up with his wife and two kids to spend most major holidays with my parents and then I go down to watch most major sporting events with him on his big screen television."

He cocked an eyebrow at me. "He's a few years older than me but we've always been pretty close. My parents live here in town."

Something on my face must have looked inquisitive because he rushed to clarify, "And no, I don't live with them."

I grinned, amused at how sensitive the idea made him.

"You really did grow up the all-American way, didn't you?" I asked.

He laughed. "*Leave it to Beaver* had nothing on my family."

I smiled at the thought. Rather than resent his life, I found myself glad to know such a childhood existed.

Without thought I asked, "Are you dating anyone?"

My question hung in the air where I could see it but couldn't grab it back again. I felt my cheeks warming as Adam cleared his throat once and then again.

"I'm not dating anyone right now," he said, licking his lips as if they were suddenly dry. "I haven't seriously dated anyone in a long time."

I felt a sense of relief and wondered why he was so uncomfortable telling me that.

Then he shifted and put his mug down. Whatever he had to say, he wanted to get it over quickly.

"Aimee, I want you to know that although I never knew Declan, I did know his sister Elyse."

His revelation was unexpected, but not shocking. After all, her grandfather had owned a house in town and I assumed she had visited it from time to time.

"Okay," I said slowly, not sure what he was trying to tell me.

His next statement suddenly made it clear.

"We dated for a few months after she dissolved her engagement with Nick."

I was surprised and a little hurt he hadn't said something before.

"You did? Why?"

He smiled and seemed to relax now that he had gotten his confession out in the open.

"Why? Because I liked her," he teased.

I shook my head and tried not to smile. I was still a little miffed.

"Okay, not why. How? How did you meet her and why did you break up?"

*And why didn't you tell me?* I silently added.

"She came here to get away and recuperate after she left Nick. I was working that summer, saving a little money before I entered the police academy in the fall. That was around eight years ago. I was only nineteen."

His eyes took on a far-away look. "She was a pretty girl and yet at the same time not really beautiful. When I met her, I remember thinking that she was a really sad person. I made her laugh and I think she appreciated that. It was never serious between us. I started school and she went back home but for the summer, it was nice."

I clarified, "That was after they broke up?"

"Right after."

"Do you know why they broke up?"

Adam cleared his throat. "We didn't talk about it much."

I frowned, suspecting there was more to the story than he was telling me.

Abruptly Adam rose from the deck chair, pulling his phone from his pocket.

"Wow! We've been talking for almost two hours! It's already eleven. We need to check on your grandfather-in-law and get you two moved to the hotel."

Shocked to realize we had been chatting that long, I grabbed our empty mugs and headed back to the house. In the kitchen I dumped them in the dishwasher, taking a moment to get it started, and then hurried to pack.

I ran into Mr. Talcos coming down the stairs with his suitcase and moved to the side to allow him to pass. He still looked tired.

After exchanging greetings, I hurried up to my room and quickly threw the rest of my toiletries with the few articles of clothing I possessed in my ragged black duffle.

I knew we were in a rush but I found myself tarrying by the window. I had opened up a lot to Adam and it left me feeling somewhat vulnerable.

Pushing aside the heavy drapery, I stood and watched the powerful waves rolling up to the shoreline. Once again its gentle repetition lulled me into a sense of peace and tranquility. Feeling slightly renewed, I turned to make my way toward the door before the black dress hanging in the closet caught my eye.

I stared at it for a moment, debating whether to pack it or not. It was a beautiful dress but it only held sad memories for me. I decided to leave it. I didn't plan on wearing it again in the near future and if I found my way back to this room, it would be waiting for me. If not, then hopefully I would be in a place that didn't require funeral attire.

## Chapter 15

My first inkling that there was a problem came as I joined the men in the foyer. Adam was talking on his cell and I overheard him sounding all business-like as I walked in with my bag strung over my shoulder.

"Okay, yep, we have a situation on our hands. I'll get them out of here as quickly as possible."

He was still speaking into the phone as he turned and eyed me approaching.

His words made me nervous and I waited as he finished his call. Hanging up, he stepped back so he could include both of us in his gaze. "It appears we have a problem."

That tinge of anxiety grew.

"Somehow Declan's death has leaked to the media and they've turned out in force to get their story."

I gasped and Mr. Talcos paled. Walking over to the living room window, I pushed aside the small white curtain covering it and glanced out. I quickly let it fall back in place. The front lawn sported no less than three grey vans with television crews setting up cameras. At the same time, a group of reporters with determined faces were making their way down the driveway and toward the house.

I glanced at Adam, feeling overwhelmed.

"No worries," he tried to reassure me. "Back-up is on their way and as soon as they clear a path, we'll have the two of you out of here."

Almost as quickly as he promised, we were barreled out of the house and directed towards an idling patrol car. Adam grabbed my hand as we started across the driveway and maintained a firm grip as we ran. I kept my eyes on the ground with my head bowed.

Questions were shouted at us and cameras were thrown in front of our faces, almost forcing us to stop.

"Was it a murder or did Declan kill himself?" one obnoxious woman shouted, her face a centimeter from mine. I must have blanched because she smiled maliciously before pulling back and thrusting a microphone in front of my face. Thankfully Adam yanked me along, away from her questions, and handed me into the waiting vehicle with Mr. Talcos right behind.

As the door closed, muffling the noise, I checked on Mr. Talcos to see how he'd fared from the onslaught. His face was grey and he looked like he was going to faint.

Stretching out a trembling hand, I placed it over his intertwined fingers and tried to smile. Together we rode, saying nothing as the cameras and voices faded away.

After a series of sharp turns, we arrived at a quaint downtown hotel. Thankfully the media hadn't followed us and we were escorted unmolested to a private suite.

Unfortunately, the hotel was only two stories high. I couldn't help wishing it were more like a city hotel with a key-access elevator to a penthouse suite, like you see on TV.

Adam came with us to the room. He looked around apologetically, and I knew he was worried about the location.

Taking my hand, he squeezed it, not letting go as he spoke, "Aimee, I have to check in with the precinct but I have an officer stationed outside. You will be fine but please don't open the door until I get back."

He stalled, eyeing Mr. Talcos before turning back to me.

"As long as the media doesn't get ahold of your location, you guys should be fine here. Please don't answer the door or the phone or go out, not even on the balcony."

I hadn't noticed yet we had a balcony. Looking across the room, I saw a sliding glass door peeking out from behind a heavy drape and a sheer curtain.

I glanced around me, taking in our surroundings. The rooms were pretty nice, spacious with a small kitchenette and two bedrooms leading off from either side of the small sitting area where we now stood. Old-fashioned wallpaper covered the walls and lace coverlets added a homey touch to the living room.

I felt warmth spreading up my arm. It was in that moment I realized Adam was still holding my hand. Looking up at him, he gave me a quick nod before squeezing and letting go.

"I'll be back with food."

I nodded.

"Stay inside," he admonished once more, not looking me in the eye, "and lock the chain latch."

I did as he said as soon as he was through the door. Turning toward Mr. Talcos, I encouraged him to pick a room and go lay down. I headed into the opposite bedroom and dumped my luggage on the white duvet covering the king sized bed. Sitting down beside it, I dropped my head into my hands and tried not to cry.

In an effort to create a distraction, I crawled to the head of the bed and reached out for the television remote laying on the bedside table. I flipped over on my back, grabbing a second pillow to put behind my head, before turning on the flat screen hanging on the far wall.

Unthinkingly I channel surfed through the basic cable package before the local news caught my eye. The malicious grin of the woman who had stuck the microphone in front of me just a half hour before accompanied a supercilious voice announcing to the world that Declan had been found dead and that the local police were investigating.

The camera then zoomed in behind her on the Talcos house as she explained that the death had occurred in the home of the deceased's grandfather. Her patronizing voice droned on and on about the crime and his death until all of a sudden my face flashed across the screen.

"Police have not yet released the identity of the woman allegedly involved with Declan Talcos. She was seen exiting the house today with Mr. Talcos, the deceased's grandfather, in what appears to be police custody. It is unknown at this time if she has been arrested and where she is being held. We will update with further news tonight at six."

The screen flashed to me being pushed into the back of the police cruiser just before going to a commercial.

Feeling nauseated, I clicked off the television. Thoughts overwhelmed me as I tried to stay focused on the case. I knew I couldn't stop people from thinking the worst, but I could try to find out the truth.

I thought about what I knew. Declan was wanted for an embezzlement that only he, his grandfather, or Howard Angle could have successfully pulled off according to Adam. Was that true? Who could confirm that for me?

I thought of Nick Santos, a man so involved in the company's financial records that he couldn't spare time for his own friend's funeral. Would he be able to tell me who else had access to the accounts? He apparently had the ability to see them.

I needed more information about the people who had known and worked with Declan. I just wasn't quite sure who to ask.

As if receiving an answer, my phone beeped. I sat up and reached down to the end of my bed, digging around in my duffle bag until I found my purse. Pulling the phone out of the side pocket, I realized that Alyssa had not only texted me three times, she had tried to call twice.

Rather than listen to her messages, I called her straight back. She answered on the first ring.

"Aimee! Are you okay? Where are you? I saw the news. What happened?" Her loud, anxious voice caused me to pull the phone away from my ear for a moment before attempting to calm her. As I went into detail about events leading up to the news spot, her voice came down an octave and we were able to regain the friendly footing from the day before.

"I just feel so bad! I think you should come down here. You have to be safer in Boston than a little seaside town like that! Our cops have experience chasing down terrorists for crying out loud. I'll call Mr. Talcos and tell him to bring you here."

I laughed. "There's just the problem that they asked me not to leave town."

I didn't get a response immediately and I guessed she was thinking.

"Well, I think you should come anyway. It's not like you're under arrest. We can let the police know where you are once you get here."

I laughed again. "Alyssa, I can't do that."

There was silence on her end of the phone and then Alyssa said slowly, "Aimee, you can't do much if you're locked up in Maine. You need to come to Boston."

I frowned at her insistence.

"You really want me to come?" I said, question more than statement.

"Yes," Alyssa said without hesitation. "There are things Erik and I want to talk to you about and we can't have this discussion over the phone."

"Can't you come here?" I asked.

Her voice lowered, "No. There's something else. Declan's old secretary, Vickie, has been acting odd."

"Declan's old secretary?" I asked, not sure who she was talking about.

"She's the one who reported Declan to the police when he first cleared out. And I think she's making plans to leave town. She emptied out her stuff and announced she has a new position in another company but I think she's leaving Boston all together. I'm not sure how much longer she'll be here, but I think you should talk to her before she goes."

"Can't you ask her why she's leaving?" I asked, not sure why I needed to talk to her.

"I tried, she just brushes me off. But you were married to Declan. I think she would talk to you. And, Aimee?"

"Yah?"

"I think she feels guilty about something."

An internal debate erupted, arguing the risk of leaving unescorted against getting information to help Declan. I knew Adam would never agree to my traipsing to Boston merely to talk to Declan's former secretary but maybe talking to her was what I needed to do.

"You think she knows more than she's saying?"

Alyssa paused before answering, "I know there's more to the story and I think she was involved. How? I don't know. But I think she'd be more willing to open up to you, since she worked for Declan."

It didn't seem likely to me at all that she would want to tell a stranger, no matter who she'd been married to, something she was hiding from the police. For whatever reason, Alyssa seemed convinced that she would.

I was evasive as I hung up the phone. I knew I shouldn't go to Boston, but at the same time if Vickie knew something and I could get it out of her, maybe I should.

Alyssa's suggestion preyed on my mind for the rest of the day. I didn't want to defy Adam, but the longer the thought of Vickie knowing something gnawed on my mind, the stronger my desire to visit Boston grew. Not only did I want to question Vickie but I wanted to see where Declan had worked and where the crime was committed. I wanted to talk to Erik; maybe even meet Nick, if I could find him.

The more I thought about it, the more it seemed the right thing to do. If I was going to help clear Declan's name, I couldn't just sit inside a hotel under police protection. Besides, Adam had asked me to stay in town. He hadn't demanded or threatened to arrest me if I left.

Since I didn't have a plan yet for escaping the hotel and getting back to my car unseen, I texted Alyssa that I was going to try to see her the following day in her office for lunch but I wasn't making any promises.

She was a little too excited and offered to come up and create a diversion while I ran out the back of the hotel into her waiting car. Convincing her that I would probably be able to make a less auspicious escape on my own was a little difficult but she agreed to wait for me in Boston.

Adam stopped by that evening with take-out and I almost changed my mind. I felt guilty deceiving him but I also knew he would never let me go. We ate practically in silence.

Excusing myself with a headache after dinner, I withdrew to my room after barely touching my supper and climbed into bed, various scenarios running through my mind.

The next morning while I prepared toast and coffee for the two of us, I simply told Mr. Talcos I was going out. He nodded, acknowledging he'd heard me, but didn't ask any questions. After putting on my jacket and checking for my keys, I boldly walked down the stairs to the front desk.

Ironically, after tossing and turning all night, escaping from the hotel was relatively easy. I failed to encounter anyone. Expecting to see at least an officer in the lobby, I stood nervously watching while the receptionist called a taxi for me without blinking an eye.

She gave me an estimated waiting time of ten minutes, so I ducked into the little hotel shop and purchased a scarf and glasses. Feeling conspicuously incognito, I covered my head and put on the shades before walking out the front doors and climbing into the taxi. No one stopped me and I couldn't believe my luck as we drove away.

Directing the driver to a house about half a mile down the street from Mr. Talcos' home, I climbed out. I waited a full minute in the driveway after he left before going around the neighbor's house, down to the beach and then back up the shoreline to where my car was parked in the Talcos driveway.

Cautiously approaching the house, I was relieved to see the area deserted. It appeared both police and media had abandoned their respective posts.

Crossing behind the back porch, I slipped along the side of the house and around the front, making a fast break for my sedan as soon as I felt the coast was clear. Graffiti still decorated the siding and I averted my eyes as I raced past.

Unlocking the car door with my key fob, I yanked it open and climbed in, my eyes darting in multiple directions. Pulling the seatbelt over my shoulder, I clicked it in place and then took a deep breath. I had never felt so devious, even when Declan and I had been on the run from the police.

The guilt grew as I started driving and I thought about how I was deceiving Adam. He had brought us food and checked on us last night because he cared, not because he had to. He easily could have sent another officer in his place. I thought about calling and just letting him know what I was planning on doing, but I couldn't. I knew without a doubt he would put a stop to it.

I was about forty-five minutes away from my destination when the phone rang. I saw on the caller ID that it was Adam and, with mixed feelings of relief and trepidation, I answered, placing it on speaker.

"Aimee?" His voice came across agitated, almost angry. "Where are you? Mr. Talcos said you left early this morning."

I could hear the worry in his voice and my guilty conscience flared.

In a small voice I replied, "I'm on my way to Declan's company to meet Erik and Alyssa for lunch."

His voice dropped lower and I knew he was upset, "You're not supposed to leave the state. I told you that. For the sake of the investigation if nothing else, but you also have an unknown person leaving you threatening notes and now the media is hounding you."

His voice rose, "What were you thinking?"

I swallowed guiltily, realizing I was no longer sure of myself. More than that, I didn't want to make trouble for him.

"Adam, I'm sorry!" I began, slowing down and pulling to the side of the road with my blinkers flashing. I picked up the phone and adjusted the setting before putting it to my ear.

"I wasn't thinking. You're right." I struggled to keep the tears from my voice, "but I need to talk to Erik and Vickie. I need to see Declan's place of work."

"Why? This isn't your case, Aimee. You're not a detective."

I gasped, his curt words freezing any concern I had for getting him in trouble by my leaving.

I could hear him breathing on the other end as he waited for my reply.

"Am I breaking the law by leaving?" I asked, my voice low and steady.

His response was terse, "No, you were in a safe house not under arrest."

I watched the cars fly by outside.

"So you're upset because my leaving will make trouble for you?"

His response was instantaneous, "Make trouble for me? It's you I'm worried about! Someone is threatening you and there's an unknown murderer out there, and you just take off by yourself? I feel like I should arrest you just to keep you where I can see you."

I didn't know what to say. His frustration masked his words but I heard the underlying sincerity in his voice. He really did care what happened to me.

Adam muttered something under his breath and I felt a warm sensation start somewhere in my middle and spread outwards.

His voice softened and lost its edge, "Why didn't you just tell me? I could have at least come with you."

"Adam, I'm sorry. Do you want me to turn around right now?" I held my breath, waiting for his answer and knowing that I would do whatever he asked.

"Where are you?" he equivocated.

"About forty minutes from my destination according to GPS."

He sighed and I waited. Finally he said, "No. Don't turn around. Have lunch with the Walshes. You're already in trouble for leaving, might as well do what you went to do."

His response surprised me and if he thought about it, I think it surprised him too.

"Do you want me to check in with you when we're done eating and again when I get back to the hotel?" I asked, wanting to find a way to reassure him.

He cracked a humorless laugh, "Yes to checking in after lunch, but I'll be at the hotel when you return."

I bit my lip. "I really am sorry, Adam. This was stupid and impulsive."

He grunted, not disagreeing but not berating me further.

"Just get back here safely," he said and then hung up. I ended the call and sat for a moment before pulling back onto the road. I was almost there.

## Chapter 16

By the time I arrived at Declan's bioresearch firm, I was stressed out. Driving in Boston was crazy and even growing up in Memphis, which I considered to be a big city, did not prepare me for the windy, twisty roads full of crazy east coast drivers. If I had been led here blindfolded and then told to drive, I would have thought I was surrounded by stereotypical New York City cabbies in a drag race.

I found a parking garage on the same street where the company was located. It was only 11:30 in the morning and I wasn't scheduled to meet up with Alyssa and Erik until noon.

Taking my time, I strolled down the sidewalk, studying the city skyscrapers towering above me on either side. People, too busy to slow their pace or share a smile, rushed past me, their lack of interest in their fellow man all too apparent.

Men and women striding by in dressy business suits made me glance down at my jeans and loose blouse with a frown. Along with my scarf and glasses, I stood out like a sore thumb.

Finally entering the building with the address I had been given, I noticed that Declan's company had nameplates occupying more than half the floors listed in the front hall. Stopping at the front desk for directions, I was directed to a row of elevators where I waited for almost ten minutes before pushing the up button.

Was I nervous? Absolutely. I didn't know exactly what I was looking for but I had an uncomfortable feeling that somehow I was crossing into dangerous territory. This is where it had all started for Declan. That idea made me shiver.

After the floor chimed and the doors opened, I stepped out into a well designed reception area. Plush chairs lined one wall while magazines were displayed on a coffee table in the middle. The opposite wall had a large screen television affixed to it.

A plump, salt and pepper haired woman sat unobtrusively at a small desk behind a glass window, almost directly in front of where the elevator opened. I stood where she could see me and waited for her to open the panel before announcing I was there to meet with Alyssa and Erik Walsh. She politely directed me to sit without inquiring who I was and picked up her phone. I could see her eyeing me through the window as she talked into the mouthpiece.

She hung up and almost immediately a door on the other side of the receptionist box swung into the room and Alyssa pranced through. Greeting me with a smile and a quick hug she ushered me back through the door and into a small hallway.

As we stepped along to what I assumed would be her office, she chatted about seeing me on television again this morning, how happy she was to see me now, and how happy Erik would be to officially meet me. We stopped outside a door with his name painted on the front and she knocked twice before opening it and stepping inside.

I followed her elegant form into the room. The man before me was the same one at the funeral with Alyssa and I was struck again by how attractive they were as a couple.

Erik indicated a small round table in the corner of his office, asking if I'd like to have a seat.

"I figured we would have more privacy here," he told me as he simultaneously pulled two chairs away from the empty table, one for me and one for his wife. She thanked him with a quick kiss and sat down. I joined her and pulled my seat up closer to the table.

I heard a ding as Erik moved to sit beside her and pulled out my phone. Adam was texting.

"Excuse me," I apologized, looking up at them.

"No problem," responded Erik, pulling out his own phone. "We ordered in and I'm just going to make sure it's still coming."

Grateful for their patience, I opened the text and read, "Make it okay?"

"Yes," I typed back, "we're just sitting down now."

"Where are you eating?" came the immediate reply.

"In Erik's office."

"Okay. Just checking."

I smiled as I shut off the screen, avoiding the urge to roll my eyes, and tucked the phone back in my purse.

I looked up to find two pairs of eyes staring at me. Feeling slightly uncomfortable, I lifted an eyebrow at Alyssa.

She smiled back at me. "Was that from a friend?"

Realizing they were curious about who I was texting, I explained about Adam and getting in trouble this morning. I finished by telling them, "Thank you both for meeting me. As you know, I think Declan was innocent. I want to find out who set him up and who killed him. Anything you can tell me would be helpful."

Alyssa's eyes filled with tears when I brought up Declan's name and Erik's steady gaze saddened.

"We're in agreement," he said, glancing at his wife. "We both knew Declan and we want to help you."

"He couldn't have done this," Alyssa broke in, wiping her eyes.

"The question is," I replied, "who could? The police think it must have been done by a person high up and intimately connected with the company."

Erik leaned back in his chair, resting his ankle across his knee.

"What do you need to know?" he asked.

I dug right in with my questions. "Who had access to all the company's financial and computer information? Or maybe even just access to Declan's? Was someone else in the company privy to his information? His secretary? An assistant manager?"

Erik cleared his throat and glanced at his wife, receiving a small nod of encouragement before turning his full attention back to me.

I sensed that what he was about to say was important.

"Declan thought someone had accessed his private accounts," he said, dropping a bombshell in my lap.

"He talked to you about this?" I asked, too shocked to ask more.

"It's what I wanted to speak to you about." His leg slipped off his knee and he changed position, leaning toward me from across the table. "Declan came to me the day he disappeared to tell me he had made some head way with the investigation. He wanted my opinion on who else could break into his accounts or possibly have access to his passwords."

"He told you someone was using his account? Who did he think it was?"

Erik shrugged. "I don't have the answer to those questions but I can tell you what I told Declan, which was anyone who was in close contact with him could probably steal his codes or password. It would just take someone who was intentionally observing him while he worked to figure out how to access his accounts. "

"Did he tell you anything else?" My mind was racing, trying to piece together what Declan had probably been working on for the two weeks we were together.

"No. He left my office that day and it was the next day I found his cell phone tucked under some paperwork. I figured then that he had deliberately left it, so I put it away until Alyssa brought it to you."

Alyssa nodded enthusiastically.

"Tell her about the phone call."

Erik cleared his throat. "I only heard from him one other time, in the middle of the night."

*That midnight phone call,* I thought, *remembering the time we had left in the middle of the night and I had waited in the car while he finished talking to someone.*

"What did he say then?" I pried, anxious to know everything.

"He told me he had discovered who had been accessing his accounts but he couldn't believe it. He wanted to substantiate his findings before coming forward and making any accusations. I got the feeling he had learned something that scared him."

My eyebrows drew together, contemplating Declan's position.

"You'd think he'd be eager to throw the blame on someone else."

"That wasn't Declan's way," Erik said simply.

Alyssa interrupted, "We think the FBI tracked that call."

I frowned. "They did?"

Erik looked sheepish. "I guess they did but I didn't know it at the time. They showed up the next day asking questions."

That explained our midnight exodus. I hadn't noticed at the time, but Declan must have ditched that phone and bought another somewhere along the way.

I thought of something else. "Why did he call you in the first place?"

Erik's face softened. "He said he was going to get to the bottom of things soon but if it turned out the way he feared, he would be leaving the country for a long time. He wanted me to take care of his grandfather."

I eyed him speculatively. "Planning to leave the country sounds either guilty of a crime or like he planned to take the blame for someone else."

Erik shrugged his shoulders and Alyssa bit her lip. I turned my attention to her and she avoided my eyes.

Looking at the table and then at Erik, she blurted out, "I always thought it involved his grandfather. He never said that but that's the only person I can think of whom he wouldn't just turn in if he found something incriminating."

I shook my head as if to clear it. I couldn't imagine Mr. Talcos as an embezzler any more than I could believe Declan was one.

Alas, suspicion began to worm its way into my consciousness. Was that why we had gone to Mr. Talcos' house? Was Declan looking for evidence to convict his grandfather? Was he planning on confronting him?

We were interrupted by a knock at the door. Erik rose to answer, revealing a woman with a sack of food and a tight-lipped smile.

Alyssa introduced her as Vickie, the secretary, and myself as Mrs. Talcos. She blinked as if taking in my name was momentarily disconcerting.

I recognized her from earlier. It was the receptionist who had sat behind the window at the front desk when I'd first arrived. Now that she wasn't hidden in a box behind glass panels, I was also able to place her from Declan's phone. She had been in the group picture I had seen with Declan and his friends sitting together at a wedding.

After a significant pause, she stepped into the room and came over to where I sat. Politely holding out her hand, she said, "I didn't realize you are Mr. Talcos' wife. I'm pleased to meet you and sorry for your loss."

I glanced at Alyssa as I shook the outstretched hand Vickie offered. Alyssa was busy with opening containers and setting out the food, so I couldn't catch her eye.

"Do you think you might have a few minutes to chat?" I asked, not beating around the bush.

A wary look came into her eyes but she didn't question my rather unusual request. "I'm not on break but maybe later we can talk if you stop by my desk."

Nodding to the other two, she turned and made a quick exit.

After the door shut, I turned to Alyssa. "That was Declan's secretary, right?"

Alyssa looked up from where she was trying to open a tub of what looked like kale salad and answered, "Yes, she was. They gave her the job out front after the blow-up."

"She's the one you wanted me to talk to?"

Alyssa smiled and nodded.

"So why didn't you invite her in to talk with us?"

Alyssa looked back down at what was definitely kale salad and scooped some onto my plate. "I already know she won't talk to me. You can try later."

Erik held his plate out for some food.

"She's the one who refused to purchase Declan's airline ticket when he wanted to leave and instead called the police, right?" I asked, still wanting to know about Vickie.

Alyssa looked surprised as if she hadn't heard that story, but Erik nodded a trifle sadly and confirmed that this was indeed the same woman.

"She was just doing what she had to do," he defended, picking up his fork and beginning to eat.

"And now she's leaving?"

"Yes. She has a better job offer supposedly."

I thought about Vickie. She had appeared nervous. Was it because I had been married to Declan? Admittedly, turning in your boss took a lot of moral courage but maybe she was still uncomfortable with her decision. I needed to find out.

## Chapter 17

After a delicious meal, I got the grand tour. I shot off a text to Adam telling him I'd text again when I was leaving. Then Erik escorted me through the halls and into a large lab while Alyssa went down one floor to her own office.

Erik explained the research being done by the firm and I had to admit that he lost me pretty much from the get-go. Not wanting to confess that I didn't know a peptide from a perpendicular angle, I listened to his detailed description from beginning to end.

It wasn't until we were nearing the end of our tour that a tall, dark man with a hooked, rather singular nose stepped out in front of us. He paused and looked our way before closing his door. He looked vaguely familiar. Then it came to me, he too had been sitting at the same table as Vickie in the wedding photo on Declan's phone.

As we approached, I saw his gaze go from my head to my toes and back again. The slight sneer that crossed his face after his blatant perusal made me uncomfortable and reminded me that I was quite obviously lacking in the business attire department. It probably couldn't be more evident that I didn't belong there.

Erik stepped toward the man and extended a hand in greeting, clearly unperturbed by the scowl on his dark features.

I really wasn't surprised to find out that this was Nick Santos. His penetrating regard as Erik introduced us to each other caused a chill to pass over me. Irrationally, the anxiety I'd felt when I'd entered the building early that morning returned.

"I knew your husband," Nick said and shock replaced my nervousness as he shook my hand lightly.

"How do you know who I am?" I stuttered in alarm. Erik had said nothing about my relationship to Declan and had simply introduced me by my first name.

He grinned as if enjoying my discomfiture and explained, "I saw you on the news. Howard told me Declan had married. When a woman was seen leaving his grandpa's house, I assumed that was her, or you, as it turns out."

I calmed down realizing his explanation was reasonable, but I still felt cautious. He was looking at me as if I was an interesting lab specimen that he wanted to observe. I had to tell myself not to squirm.

Trying to shake off my nerves, I asked Erik if we were going to meet Alyssa for coffee before I took off again. Erik immediately started telling me about the café in the basement and invited Nick to join us.

He accepted and the three of us made our way down in the elevator. While Erik remained outside calling Alyssa, Nick and I went inside the cute little coffee shop and got in line.

There were only one or two people in front of us and I tried to make polite small talk while we waited. Unthinkingly, I asked Nick how he knew Declan, only remembering a second too late that he had once been Elyse's fiancée.

Nick seemed unaffected by my question and brushed it off, saying they went back a long way.

"So how do you know Declan?" he asked, casually turning toward me as we advanced in line. "I feel like he should have at least mentioned he was seeing someone before he went off and got married."

His voice was congenial but the hard glint in his eyes contradicted the light tone with which he spoke. I hemmed and hawed to come up with an answer, relief rushing over me as the barista called me up to the counter. I hurried to request a mocha latte, reluctant to disclose to Nick Santos how unusual my marriage had been.

By the time I collected my drink, I had regrouped. Nick was one of the people I needed to question and for a few minutes at least, I had the opportunity to talk to him alone.

Looking around, I saw a table near the wall with four vacant chairs. Holding my paper cup, I claimed it and waited for Nick to join me.

"Mr. Talcos mentioned you," I began as he sat down. "He told me you've known the family for years."

"That I have," he said, sitting in the chair closest to me and nudging it forward, "so you understand why I am surprised Declan never mentioned you."

I sighed and realized that if I was going to get anywhere, I was going to have to appease his curiosity. Using the abridged version, I recounted how I had met Declan and married him. Surprisingly, Nick didn't seem to find it that odd of a story.

"Declan must have trusted you, to marry you while he was on the run."

I murmured in agreement, sipping the foam and chocolate cooling in front of me.

"It must have been quite a love match."

I looked up, caught off guard by the personal inference. Not wanting to give in to his nosiness, I nodded and said nothing.

We were silent for a moment before I started my own inquiry. By this time, I could see Erik waiting to collect his order and knew my time with Nick was limited.

"Nick, can I ask you a delicate question?"

Nick looked surprised and interested. He nodded and leaned toward me, his big nose even more striking up close.

"Of course. What would you like to know?"

"Do you think Declan was responsible for the embezzlement? Mr. Talcos told me you have the ability to see all the accounts and transactions so you of all people would have the best idea how the money was taken." I waited breathlessly, hoping that he would answer me in the negative, hoping he would confirm his faith in Declan's innocence.

Instead his eyes darkened and the corners of his mouth drooped.

"I wish I could say I didn't think that. I've known Declan a long time and honestly, as a friend and boss, he's the last person I would have suspected. But the books don't lie and there's not much else you can think, when you have the evidence right in front of you."

I was about to delve further into this alleged incontrovertible proof when Erik set down two steaming mugs on the table.

"Alyssa will be down shortly. She's just finishing up." He took the seat on the other side of me and rather than pursue our previous discussion, I let the two men carry the conversation.

"So how are things looking from your end?" Erik directed his inquiry toward Nick who now sat stiffly in his chair.

Nick answered briefly, "Not finding much. The FBI thinks they have everything wrapped up. Should be out of our hair in a couple more days."

Erik frowned but didn't answer. His tie was askew.

I studied Nick, remembering the other probing question I'd had, "The day before Declan disappeared from the company he had a meeting with you. Do you remember it?"

Nick gave me a strange look, his hooked nose lifting slightly, and shook his head.

"Declan mentioned meeting with me?" he asked, misunderstanding and looking slightly worried. "I don't remember it. Did he say what the meeting was about?"

"No, not at all," I said, ignoring the fact that he thought Declan was the one who had told me about the meeting, "I was wondering if you could tell me."

I paused, hoping he wouldn't see through my awkward attempt to solicit information about something I really knew nothing about.

Alyssa chose that moment to join us. She greeted Nick, giving him a quick hug, and I was reminded of the history these three people shared. They had worked together and known the Talcos family for over a decade. I had known Declan for little more than two weeks.

I spent the rest of the coffee hour listening to the others talk shop, trying not to feel defeated by Nick telling me he believed Declan to be the embezzler. By the time we finished, it was well past three in the afternoon. I made an excuse about wanting to beat rush hour traffic and stood to leave. As I did, Nick reached out and touched my wrist.

"Aimee, I wanted to say I'm sorry about what happened to Declan." He hesitated, looking genuinely concerned. "And, well, as more comes to light, if you need anything, I'd like to help you."

I looked down at his hand still resting on my forearm and then up at him. His sincerity surprised me but I thanked him politely before leaving the cafe.

Alyssa followed and caught up with me at the elevator. She accompanied me to the vestibule of the building to say goodbye. Before we parted, she gave me a tight hug and told me that she was glad I came. The angst from Nick telling me Declan was guilty began to lessen.

As I stepped back from the hug, I suddenly remembered that I had told Vickie, the secretary, that I would stop by to talk with her on my way out. I waited for Alyssa to go before I made an about face and headed back to the elevator.

I rode back up to Erik's floor and got out like before. This time when I went up to the glass, the seat behind it was empty and no one was in sight. I knocked lightly and waited but no one came. Noticing that the time was dangerously approaching rush hour, I slid the glass open and grabbed a sticky note from the desk. Looking around and still not seeing anyone, I jotted a message and left my number, asking Vickie to call me.

Closing the window, I wondered briefly if I should wait longer but the idea of driving home after dark made me nervous. After one last glance, I left to find my car.

## Chapter 18

The first thing I did when I got to my car was text Adam that I was fine and that I was headed home. I didn't get an immediate response so I closed out the messages app and slipped the phone into a cup holder, the GPS already programmed and ready to go.

As I left town, the sky dark and grey up ahead, I realized I was driving into a rainstorm. Already small droplets pelleted my windshield. As visibility worsened, I questioned my judgment in making this impulsive trip in the first place. Now, if anything, I was more confused and even a little afraid. Nick, besides making me nervous and uncomfortable, frustratingly confirmed what everyone already believed: that Declan was the only one who could have stolen the money.

The rain picked up and my thoughts turned to Erik and Alyssa's theory that Declan was protecting someone. I could understand their reasoning but who? And would that person kill him in return? Declan was the kind of guy to face the music, not run from it.

I thought about the people closest to Declan. Besides his grandfather, could he have suspected Howard Angle, Erik or even Alyssa? I struggled to understand. Declan's attempt to leave the country just didn't jive with him being on the verge of discovering the embezzler.

Just after I crossed the border into Maine while making my way through a rather desolate area, an eighteen-wheeler passed me in the fast lane. A large sheet of water sprayed up, covering my windshield in a wave of dirty fluid, momentarily blinding me. I stupidly slammed on my brakes, my old, practically treadless tires causing me to hydroplane. My anti-lock brakes began to click and for a second I thought that I was coming out of what had become a fishtail.

Suddenly, I was struck from behind, my car propelled sideways and then spinning off the road.

The saying, "I felt my life flash before my eyes" became a reality as I literally felt like my car was revolving in slow motion, memories of years past flying rapidly through my mind.

I began a bumpy descent down an incline until the front end of my car caught on something tall, dark and solid, whirling me one last time into what I later found out was a tree.

My vehicle struck the wooden object with the front passenger door and I was thrown first right and then left. The initial impact on my front end had caused my airbags to deploy and the second impact now caused the side ones to go off.

I sat for a moment in shock, not quite believing it was over. The windshield was in pieces and I was covered in glass. My car smelled funny and I felt something cold trickling down my face. My first movement was to touch my forehead, checking to see if I was okay.

As I reached up I felt pain and I pulled my hand back. I saw in the quickly waning daylight that I had dark red blood covering my fingers. For a moment I was lightheaded and wondered if I would be sick.

Trying to regain control, I breathed deeply and refused to look at my hand. I visually searched around the damaged interior for my cell phone. Seeing it had flown out of the cup holder and onto the floor in front of the passenger seat, I reached over and grabbed it. My left shoulder screamed in protest, the slightest pressure from moving against the seatbelt enough to make me feel like it had been ripped off.

Straightening up, I took a deep breath and tried to think calmly. I contemplated undoing my seatbelt and getting out of the damaged car before thinking better of it. I turned on my phone to find Adam's name. I needed to call for help first.

Leaning my throbbing crown back against the headrest, I waited for him to answer. One ring. Two rings. Three.

Rain continued to pelt my car, wetting me through the broken windshield, and making me realize I was getting cold. As I waited for Adam to pick up, I figured out I could move both of my hands but I still couldn't lift my left arm.

The phone was starting the fifth ring when he finally answered.

"Why do you always take so long to pick up?" I asked, my voice weak but querulous.

"Aimee? Are you okay?" he asked, ignoring my rudeness.

I took a deep breath so I wouldn't break down crying and started to tell him what had happened. I began to cry anyway.

His alarm was evident but he quickly took charge. He told me to turn off the engine but keep my headlights on, high beams if possible, and the hazard lights. I hadn't even realized the engine was still running.

He put me on hold while he called EMS and state highway patrol. When he came back on I was beginning to feel sleepy.

"Aimee, where do you hurt?" his question broke through my the fog in my brain.

I struggled to answer him, my voice fading as my eyes closed, "I'm not sure. My head hurts. My shoulder hurts. I haven't tried to get up yet. I feel kinda woozy."

His immediate response was to tell me to sit tight. "Unless the car is on fire, I want you stay in your seat. Don't even remove your seatbelt."

I glanced down, surprised to see the belt still in place. Hadn't I released that already? Or had I just thought about undoing it?

"I'll be there in thirty minutes. If the ambulance gets you loaded before I get there, go with them and I'll meet you at the hospital."

"You're a little bossy," I said drowsily. "Are you always bossy like this?"

I heard him laugh softly and I wished whole-heartedly that I had remained in Maine like he'd told me.

The next thing I knew firefighters and EMTs were outside my car, gently working to extract me and all the while talking reassuringly. They put a brace on my neck and took the phone from me. Adam stayed on the line but we were no longer talking. More than anything I wanted to sleep. Once safely lifted into the ambulance, everything faded away.

Adam met me at the hospital. The ambulance had brought me with lights and sirens blazing and if I didn't have such a big headache and feel like I could barely keep my eyes open, I would have died of embarrassment.

The next few hours passed in a haze and by the time my hairline was stitched, my shoulder reduced and I had passed all my other tests, I was finally starting to feel more like myself.

Unfortunately I was also myself on pain medication, which made for interesting conversation.

Opening my eyes as the anesthesia from fixing my dislocated shoulder was wearing off, I looked up to see Adam standing beside my stretcher, concern and worry etched on his face. I tried to smile in reassurance but I think it came across more like a grimace because he frowned.

Seeing I was awake, he reached out and stroked my cheek with his thumb, and even in my drugged state, I knew I liked his touch.

"You can do that all day," I said, starting to close my eyes again and then gasped, my eyes flying wide open. "Did I just say that aloud?"

Adam's smile grew and I could see his blue eyes twinkle. There was a five o'clock shadow on his face and he looked like he hadn't slept in days.

"Yes, you did and it's going on record."

"I can't get away with anything," I complained, my eyes drawn to his. His expression became serious and he stilled his hand.

"Can you tell me anything about the accident? The police report says that no one saw it and no one reported it until I called it in. What happened?"

My forehead wrinkled as I struggled to remember the details and that, unfortunately, reminded me that I had a lovely wound decorating my noggin. I reached up, relieved to feel the stitches running along my hairline.

Adam noticed my apparent concern and teased, "Don't worry. The scar won't be noticeable."

His hand took mine, pulling it away from my face, and he moved it down to rest on the hospital sheet.

Relaxing, I tried my best to tell him what had happened. Except for the semi-truck passing me and ruining my visibility, there really wasn't much to say.

"I think I hydroplaned. And then I felt this impact from behind, which pushed me off the road and over the edge, I guess."

"You took out a guardrail," Adam told me, his gaze serious. "You're lucky you didn't flip. Did you see who hit you?"

"No," I said, chagrined. "It must have been a vehicle coming from behind but I honestly have no idea who they were. Maybe they hydroplaned too."

I finished my narrative sorry I couldn't be more helpful.

Adam looked thoughtful. "Interesting, no other accidents were reported tonight."

I watched him, trying to understand what he was saying. "Do you think it was intentional?"

Adam shrugged. "Or someone scared they'd get in trouble," he said, then he lowered his voice as if speaking to himself, "but you would think a half-way decent person would have checked on you or at least reported that you needed help at the soonest opportunity."

I nodded sagely, my mind affected by the drugs. "You would think."

Not feeling upset in the least, I wondered, *Was someone trying to run me off the road? Was this related to the case?*

Then I looked down and saw my left arm in a sling.

"How long do I need this?" I asked, indicating the thing strapped to my body.

"I'm not sure," Adam answered, his brow clearing. "The doctor said he'd be back after you woke up. I'm not even sure if you're going to be allowed to go home or if they're going to keep you."

At that exact moment, I wasn't sure what I wanted. I had a strong desire to return to the hotel and Mr. Talcos, but I was also rather doubtful I could walk.

I spent the next forty-five minutes slowly bringing Adam up to date in regards to my time in Boston. While I talked, he held the hand of my good arm loosely, occasionally rubbing my palm with his thumb.

"Well, I'm not glad it happened," he said when I was finished, "but if you had to have an accident, I'm glad it happened on this side of the Maine state line."

"Would you have gotten in trouble if I was in Massachusetts?" I asked, suddenly aware that Adam might have been jeopardizing his job by letting me go.

"Not any more," he said, still rubbing my hand. "I took myself off the case. I'm officially on vacation for the next two weeks."

I turned my hand over to stop his caress and carefully gazed up at him. He looked at me intently, concern and something else on his handsome face.

"Why?"

"It became too personal. And when I realized I had just told you to go to Boston if you needed to, well, I knew I was no longer impartial. I can't work your case if I can't follow the rules."

"What does that mean?"

"That means, for the next two weeks, if you want me to, I will help you. Just not in an official capacity."

I looked at him steadily, taking in what he had just told me, the drugs still messing with my mind. A feeling of contentment filled my heart and maybe something more, like a little bit of happiness.

"Does this mean you think Declan might not have done it?" I asked, squeezing his hand.

He tightened his grip, "It means I'm keeping an open mind and it means I want to make sure you're safe."

I closed my eyes, not wanting him to know how he made me feel. I was drifting off to sleep when the doctor came back in the room, blustering and saying how lucky I was.

I looked down at Adam's fingers, still holding mine, and thought that I didn't need him to tell me that. I knew I was blessed.

The doctor didn't have much to say otherwise. He explained that I had a concussion and had dislocated my shoulder. Apparently I had signed a permission form for the procedure they had already performed and I found it odd that I couldn't remember doing that.

"The stitches should come out in five days," he said, "and if someone promises to keep an eye on you over the next couple days, I'll release you tonight."

I looked over at Adam who winked at me while answering the doctor, "All week if I have to."

I turned back to the doctor with my cheeks flushed and asked to be discharged. I wasn't sure I was ready for this side of Adam.

It only took thirty more minutes before I was up for discharge. They tried to return my blouse to me, still damp and covered with bloodstains, but I had seen the last of that exact piece of clothing and had the nurse throw it away. Instead I kept the johnny and scrub bottoms to wear home.

Discharge paperwork in hand and a tech wheeling me outside, I was ready to get out of there. Adam met us at the door, his car just outside. He draped his rain jacket over my shoulders, as there was still a steady downpour, and then ran around to open the car door while the aide wheeled me closer.

Adam helped me inside, commenting on my bare feet before going around and climbing into the driver's seat. I wondered what had become of my shoes before having a plastic bag with them thrust in front of me.

I took it from the aide who quickly shut me inside and then placed it at my feet. Adam pulled the seatbelt across me, securing it before turning and putting on his own. Then he turned on the car, shifted into drive and we started for home.

As we exited the parking lot, I turned and asked him, "That reminds me, what about my car? Is it totaled?"

Adam frowned and glanced at me, perhaps gauging how well I could take it, before focusing on the road.

"The police had it towed and from what they said, it doesn't look good. The report's in my wallet. I'll give it to you when we get to the hotel."

I laid my head back on the seat and closed my eyes, wondering if I had blanked out signing that too.

It was past midnight and the rain continued to come down with a soft pattering. Excusably, the sound put me to sleep.

I was awakened by Adam, softly repeating my name, almost half an hour later as he released my belt.

He climbed out and then came around to gently assist me from the car and guide me into the hotel, leaving it idling in the front entry. As I ascended the one flight of stairs with half open eyes, all I could focus on was getting to bed.

A police officer stood guard outside the room when we arrived. Adam greeted him and asked when the next officer would be out. After learning that wouldn't be until the next morning, Adam fished my keycard out of my purse and used it to open the door. It came as a surprise to realize the police or EMS had retrieved my purse from the scene of the accident.

"When did we get a guard outside the door?" I asked as Adam helped me cross the threshold.

He slowly walked me just inside the doorway of my bedroom.

"This morning," he said, giving me a look, "after you left."

He stood there distractedly for a moment and I wondered what he was waiting for. Then he looked awkwardly over my shoulder and asked if I needed help getting ready for bed.

I told him I wasn't planning on doing anything but going to sleep, which seemed to relieve him. It must have been the medication still on board, but I giggled.

Smiling a little, he gently pulled me close for a hug. Then he dropped a kiss on my forehead, careful to avoid the suture line, before letting me go and backing out into the main suite.

"I'm glad you're okay. Get a good night's rest." He reached out and then let his hand fall. "I'll be over tomorrow morning. The new detective, his name is Irons, will probably be here too."

Then he was gone.

After Adam left, I turned toward my bed but then remembered I should lock the front door. I painfully ambled, still dizzy from the medication and head injury, to slide the bolt. Thankfully this was accomplishable with one hand.

I thought about checking on Mr. Talcos in the other bedroom but didn't want to wake or scare him. I was glad he hadn't waited up for me.

After collapsing under the covers, I thought I would go right to sleep, but my face and head itched. Making my way to the bathroom, I panicked with one glance at my face. Dried blood mixed with brown iodine crusted my forehead and dripped down to my neck. I was able to reach most of it with a washcloth but when I tried to undo the sling strapped to my body to clean where blood had dripped on my chest, I had to quit. Every movement hurt and the band just seemed to squeeze tighter.

Realizing it was an exercise in futility, I threw the rag into the bathtub. I ran a toothbrush over my teeth, then dropped half dead onto the mattress and closed my eyes for almost ten hours.

## Chapter 19

I woke up with my mouth full of cotton and my head pounding. A soft knock on the door alerted me to the presence of someone just outside.

Feeling like I'd been hit by a truck, I painstakingly scooted to the side of the bed and sat up. Instinctively, I knew that was as far as I was going to get.

I tried calling out to whoever was at the door, but my throat was hoarse and now my head was spinning.

Unable to speak louder, I whispered, "Who's there?"

Adam's soft voice carried through, "It's me. Can I come in? I've got some medicine for you."

I looked down at the johnny I still wore and realized that at some point during the night I had lost the one snap that held it together over my injured shoulder. I pulled the front a little higher, tucking part of it under the strap on my neck and threw the open sleeve over my collarbone towards my back.

"Yes," I answered, hoping I was decent.

The door slowly opened and Adam stood there, showered, shaved and looking disconcertingly handsome. Knowing my face was swollen and bruised and there was blood caking my hair, I felt embarrassed and tried to ignore his probing stare.

Entering the room, he walked over and solicitously inquired how I felt. He had a couple tablets and handed them to me along with a glass of water.

"I picked up your prescription this morning. I figured you could use something a little stronger than Tylenol for the first day or so."

I swallowed the pills gratefully and then sipped on the water. Adam moved around the bed, opening the light-damping, heavy drapes but leaving the lighter, white shears closed. Squinting my eyes at the bedside clock, I could make out that it was after noon.

"Does the light bother you?" Adam asked, coming back to me and looking at my face in concern.

"Not any worse than without it," I answered truthfully.

He stood for a moment, not saying anything.

"Do you want me to ask a female officer to come up and help you bathe?" he finally asked, avoiding my eyes.

I smiled for the first time that morning and the movement made my cheeks hurt. Apparently I had more bruises than I realized.

"If you can take this sling off me, I think I can shower and dress on my own."

Adam gave me a measured look before advancing to my side and unstrapping the Velcro on my back. I understood why I had so much trouble with it the night before as it came loose. My arm part was strapped to a large fabric swathe that went around my chest.

His voice was husky as he murmured, "You have some serious bruises forming back here."

With the slack of the released Velcro, I felt the johnny slipping. Quickly grabbing and holding the corner in place, I pulled away from Adam's cool touch, rushing over my words to tell him I could handle the rest.

He looked nervous when he stepped away, rubbing the back of his neck with one hand and looking at the door.

"Detective Irons should be here in half an hour. Mr. Talcos is up. Call if you need anything," he said awkwardly. I watched him turn and almost run from the room. Then I sat on the side of the bed, waiting for the pain meds to kick in.

It was slow going but I was able to shower, wash and even comb my hair on my own. I took the dressing down one-handed from my face and looked at the cut for the first time.

The laceration was pretty extensive. It stretched from along the hairline just left of the center of my forehead for a good five or six inches. The edges looked red and angry and the large purple bruise that accompanied it was already working its way toward my left eyebrow. Another bruise decorated my left cheek and I imagined that the impact that had dislocated my arm had also caused this.

My arm actually felt okay as long as I didn't move it too much. Sliding it carefully through a short-sleeved button down shirt, I struggled to close it with my good hand. I didn't even attempt to put the intricate sling back on.

Feeling refreshed after bathing and with pain meds on board, I made my way into the central living space where I found both men waiting for me.

Adam and Mr. Talcos stood as I entered, Mr. Talcos coming forward to kiss my cheek and offer words of sympathy and concern. He was looking better today and I was glad to see that at least one of us was recovering from the stress of the murder and our sudden media fame.

Adam made me sit down and brought me a light lunch. I hadn't regained my appetite so I just picked at my food as they talked over me.

I had just put down my spoon after taking another bite of the rich tomato soup when Detective Irons knocked. He was a robust man with a big mustache and made short work of our interview.

"I've read through all your notes." He nodded at Adam as if it wasn't odd to have the former head of the investigation now present as a bystander. "And I think I've got a handle on what's happened. For now we're going to work on protecting you and in return," he cocked a big bushy eyebrow at me, "I need you to promise not to leave the hotel again."

I sheepishly agreed and after a quick run through of my escapades from the night before, he took off.

I was gearing up to go back to my room, tired from the short but draining interview, when Mr. Talcos spoke up.

"My dear," he began, "I wanted to tell you I met with my lawyer yesterday."

"Here?" I asked, surprised. Apparently I wasn't the only one breaking the rules.

Adam's glance flickered to me and he winked. "He went through the proper channels and got permission *before* he made the appointment."

I nodded, chastised, but relieved at the same time. I was glad that Adam could tease me about it.

"What did you meet about?" I asked, turning back to Mr. Talcos.

His grey eyes regarded me seriously. "Declan's estate for one thing and what he left you. Also we'll need legal counsel if the FBI is going to press charges posthumously or involve us with their investigation of the embezzlement."

I coolly nodded in understanding but my insides quaked.

"We were only married for three days," I brought up, trying to calm my racing heart, "I don't deserve to benefit from our marriage."

Mr. Talcos looked hesitant, as if choosing his words carefully. He seemed to struggle with what he wanted to say.

"Aimee," he began, my name spoken softly in his wheezy voice, "I know your marriage was one of convenience." He looked over at Adam as if ascertaining that this information wasn't a surprise, then continued, "I also know that something deeper occurred to unite you with my grandson."

I started to protest and Mr. Talcos held up a hand to stop me.

"Maybe not physically," he said and I blushed at his statement, looking down at my soup self-consciously.

He continued unabashed, "But you were there for him when he was at his lowest point and believed in him when no one else did. You trusted him and helped him when he needed it most, which to me shows you cared more for him than anyone else."

Everything had gone silent in the room and I looked up to see Mr. Talcos had tears in his eyes.

His voice choked as he went on, "Including me. Until you showed up at my house with him, I thought Declan had gone crazy, sabotaged my company and left the country."

I saw the sorrow on his face and realized the guilt he had been carrying for judging his grandson so harshly.

"It wasn't until he was dead that I knew he would never betray me or rob his own company. I also know that if he was alive today, he would still be taking care of you and wanting to know you were provided for. I'm not asking you to take over his estate, but I do want you to accept the comfort being his widow should provide."

His expression was paternal as he waited for my reaction. I didn't have an answer for him.

He continued, "We can work out a monthly stipend for you to live on and put the rest into the company stocks or savings, whatever you prefer. Declan, aside from his part ownership of our company, is leaving you over thirty million dollars."

I felt like someone had sucker-punched me. I literally couldn't breathe for a moment. It was an amount of money that in my wildest dreams I couldn't imagine anyone possessing, least of all me.

Mr. Talcos watched patiently, giving me time to recover. I didn't know what to say and so I just sat there, breathing deeply and trying to calm down.

I felt Adam stiffen in the chair next to me and I knew inherently that this was going to affect our new and tenuous relationship. I glanced at him out of the corner of my eye as Mr. Talcos started speaking again.

"Of course, everything will be on lock-down until the investigation is concluded. Until that time I intend to provide you with anything you need."

My mind whirled, barely hearing what more was said. My soup had grown cold and I realized I had no desire to finish it.

Putting it aside, I turned to look at the man I was coming to care for, the same man who had taken himself off the case because he felt his feelings for me biased him. Adam's expression was blank and at first he refused to meet my eye. When he finally did it was like looking into the face of a stranger. The rebuff went through me like a knife.

Precipitously I decided I needed to go back to bed and rest, but mostly because I just wanted to be alone. Ignoring the pain in my body, I inched forward to the edge of my seat, saying in a faltering voice that I needed to lay down.

Immediately Adam was there, assisting me to stand. His expression was solicitous but his eyes were cold and reserved. No one would believe this was the same man who had stayed by my side in the hospital, holding my hand and stroking my face.

It dawned on me that in finding out I was incredibly wealthy, I had just alienated the one person who was fast becoming the most important person in my life.

When we got back to the room, Adam insisted on helping me replace the sling over my clothes. His touch was impersonal and he continued to avoid eye contact. After letting me know he'd return in the evening to check on us, he left.

The door closed quietly behind him and in the silence he left behind, I felt like he was simultaneously closing the door on our barely budding relationship. Ice wrapped around my heart and I worried that the change I sensed in Adam was not something that would easily pass.

Then, just like that, the ice melted and the pain from everything that had transpired in the last twenty-four hours hit me. I cried myself to sleep.

## Chapter 20

The next twenty-four hours passed quietly with Adam avoiding me. At least he hadn't completely disappeared. He was still there later that afternoon when I woke up and he came back the next morning. As usual, he was considerate when we were together, but something had changed. His attention was no longer personal and I was beginning to think he was trying to avoid even looking at me.

Mr. Talcos, on the other hand, seemed relieved to have me back. I think the car accident really affected him, as if he realized that because of my relationship with Declan, I was all he had left of a family.

He even asked me if I would consider calling him grandfather. At first I balked, as the term was intimate and I didn't feel that I deserved to be treated like I was a relative. Eventually I agreed to think about it as I could see that it would not only make him happy, but it helped to alleviate some of the guilt he carried over from doubting Declan.

Knowing it was a painful subject, I avoided bringing up why he had thought Declan was involved. However, several evenings later as the two of us sat eating supper alone, he abruptly said, "You know, I didn't suspect Declan without cause."

The remote expression in his eyes made me wonder what he was talking about and I had to focus my wandering mind in order to understand what he was saying. Of course, I had been thinking about Adam.

"I was told he was guilty. Howard Angle called me the day before Declan disappeared to tell me that the FBI had tracked the embezzled money as far as they could. It had passed out of the company through Declan's access codes and into a seldom-used bank account that I had access to. Howard was worried that I would be implicated but he was even more worried that Declan was involved. Who else would have access to Declan's passwords and my accounts? Unfortunately, by the time the FBI tracked the money to my account, all of it had been transferred into untraceable foreign banks."

His unexpected revelation took me aback. No one had told me just how the embezzlement had occurred and as I turned over what Mr. Talcos had said, I felt the same helpless feeling he obviously did when he shared these details with me: Who else had access if not Declan?

I came out of my reverie to see him watching me closely, sorrow marring his countenance. I quickly tried to reassure him and alleviate any guilt he had for doubting Declan.

"It makes perfect sense," I pointed out. "Of course you suspected him. But now that we agree he couldn't have done it, that just means we have to look harder for who did."

He grunted and went back to eating.

I don't think I made him feel any better but at least I tried.

Adam stopped by later to check on us. We sat and talked with Mr. Talcos until around nine when that elderly gentleman announced he was going to bed.

Adam rose to leave also, but I reached out and touched his arm lightly, stalling him.

"Please stay," I asked, my tone embarrassingly close to begging. "We need to talk."

He looked hesitant but then dropped into the seat across from where I sat on the sofa, noticeably as far away from me as he could get.

He had mellowed out somewhat since discovering I was an heiress but he was still distant. At times I would catch him watching me but then he would quickly look away. We had yet to talk about my inheritance and for me it was beginning to feel like the proverbial elephant in the room.

I heard rather than saw the door to Mr. Talcos' room close and I opened the conversation by recounting what he had told me earlier regarding Declan and the use of his passwords.

Adam listened to me intently, but I got the feeling that he already knew how the embezzlement had been transacted. When I was done, he stood and paced the room before coming to sit beside me. I looked at him, surprised he had willingly sat so close. I studied his face, unsuccessfully trying to get a read on his feelings.

When his voice came it was deep and startled me out of my own thoughts.

"I can understand why Mr. Talcos thought his grandson was involved; it would be rather hard to believe otherwise."

"It just doesn't make sense," I shot back, my feathers ruffling with the implied accusation. "It's just too easy a path to trace, at least on this side of the equation. If he had planned to steal three billion dollars, he would have had to leave the minute he took the money. The only way he could have pulled off the embezzlement successfully is if he had disappeared before the money was found missing."

Adam nodded, one finger tapping his chin in thought. I could tell he was listening to me.

"Someone must have used Declan and his grandfather to pull this off, someone close enough to gain access to their accounts," I continued. "The question is who?"

"The million dollar question," he responded thoughtlessly and then winced. I stared at him for second.

"The inheritance really bothers you, doesn't it?" I asked softly, trying to get to the heart of the problem.

He looked away, not meeting my eye and not responding to my question.

"Adam, look at me. We need to talk about this."

He was making me worried.

Finally, he turned to face me with a wary expression.

"What's wrong?" I asked, a feeling of desperation rising within me. "Is it the money? Is it my marriage to Declan? What? You've been practically ignoring me for three days now!"

Adam looked uncomfortable and opened his mouth to speak. He closed it again without saying anything, shaking his head as if searching for words.

Finally, he leaned towards me and spoke, "Aimee, when I took myself off the case it was because I realized I was no longer impartial. I felt a connection to you and I cared too much for what you thought in order to remain objective."

I nodded, liking what he was saying but not understanding what it had to do with his recent behavior.

"What does that have to do with the last three days?" I finally asked.

Adam looked flustered. "The money changes that, changes what could be between us."

I broke in, "What? How?"

His pained expression made me wince. "Aimee, I make a little more than fifty thousand dollars a *year*. As Declan's widow, you could collect that in a week."

He shut his eyes and leaned back. "That puts us on totally different footing, unequal footing."

I shook my head, not comprehending. "No, it doesn't! I don't come from money. I've never asked for it and I don't plan on living a life of opulence. If anything, I'll give it to charity or something like that in Declan's memory."

He smiled at me sympathetically. "You can't spend that much on charity. No one can. And you should have a life of ease. Mr. Talcos was right; you were faithful to Declan, during his lifetime and now in death by trying to clear his name. You deserve to spend the rest of your life taken care of by him."

My eyes narrowed. "You're saying I deserve to live my life alone with the money of a dead man for comfort?"

He looked uncomfortable. "No, what I'm saying is that now you will be thrust into a different world. You will associate with other wealthy people. You'll probably meet someone with the same social status and realize that's the sort of man you want in your life."

His cheeks flamed red as he sat stiffly, reading off his reasons as from a list.

"Or I'll find a treasure hunter," I said, crossing my arms. Why was I even arguing with this stubborn and annoying man?

"And as time goes on," he continued staring off into space, the blush fading "you'll see that our worlds would never mesh."

"You don't know that," I huffed.

"Do you know why Elyse and I only had a summer fling?" he asked. "How I knew it would never go any further?"

He paused, waiting for an answer I couldn't give, "Because she told me it wouldn't. She told me she could never marry someone who wasn't financially equal to her because she would always wonder if it was her or her money they wanted."

I shook my head again, not wanting to hear this. "I think you're being ridiculous. It's just money."

*And I'm not Elyse,* I defiantly added to myself.

His expression tensed and he leaned in. "Do you want to know why Nick and Elyse broke up? It was because she came across a letter he had written to a college buddy, bragging about what he was going to do with her money once he married her. It broke her heart."

"How sad. Why didn't you tell me before?" I asked, my voice softening.

Adam shook his head and looked down. "She told me in confidence. I didn't feel right repeating it."

I watched the emotions play across his face.

"You were falling in love with her," I said, understanding dawning.

Adam turned and pulled away.

"I liked her," he said. "I wouldn't go that far."

"Then why are you still so upset about something that happened eight years ago?"

I watched as he struggled with his thoughts.

Finally he turned toward me.

"This!" He pointed at me and then towards himself. "Whatever is going on, is little more than a chemical attraction between two people thrown into difficult circumstances. It's not real and if we react to it, we're both just going to end up hurt."

The pragmatic words were said harshly and as I watched, a cold mask dropped over the Adam I was coming to know.

Something broke inside me and in that moment I knew that what I felt for Adam was much stronger than a mere physical attraction; his rejection cut to my core and I could think of nothing to say in reply.

I turned away, unsuccessfully trying to hide my face as tears filled my eyes.

"Aimee," he whispered softly above my ear.

He was much closer than I had realized, "Look at me."

He took my chin in his hand and gently turned my face until I had to meet his eyes.

Tears erupted and began to slide silently down my cheeks. I couldn't stop them.

"I'm sorry," he sighed, using his thumb to gently wipe away another tear. "I don't want to hurt you."

"It's a little late for that," I whispered, my voice breaking embarrassingly.

At this, I began to cry in earnest. Groaning, Adam pulled me towards him, careful of my injuries, and then held me, stroking my back, and letting me cry.

"Its just money," I said, pulling back from his chest and sniffling a short while later. "Some day the truth will be known, you'll be working another case and I'll be sitting home all alone, counting my money."

I knew my face was now purple, red and splotchy. At this point, I didn't blame Adam for wanting to back out of a potential relationship with me. Instead, he smiled, his eyes lighting up, and he tucked a lock of hair behind my ear.

"You're telling me to stop worrying about the future, aren't you?"

I nodded. "And have a little more faith."

He pulled me toward him again and for a split second I thought he was going to kiss me, but instead he rested his chin on top of my head, careful of my stitches, and settled me sideways against his chest.

I sighed, confused and still unsure where we stood, but willing to keep things like they were.

His hand gently stroked my good arm. "I think you need to get some sleep," he said, the motion gradually stilling.

I nodded in agreement, but didn't make a move to get up. We sat for a few minutes longer.

"Do you think whoever did this will come after Mr. Talcos next?" I asked, the fingers of my right hand reaching up and tangling in his.

"No, why?" he asked, sounding surprised at my random question.

"Well, he's the only other person who was close to Declan."

Adam's hand tightened on mine. "Nothing has happened to make me think he's in danger. You're the one they seem to be after."

I nodded reluctantly, a crazy idea popping into my head. "Hey! Maybe we could use me to draw out whoever it is. I mean if they want to get to me, we could make it easy. Maybe even make them think I know more than I do."

Adam's voice was firm and he didn't hesitate. "Absolutely not."

I pulled away and looked up at him. "But how else are we going to find the murderer? No one has disappeared like you'd expect the embezzler to do. We really have no way of finding out who it is unless we flush them out, make them think we know more than we do."

Adam frowned at me. "Have you been watching cop shows?"

I imitated his grimace and shook my head. "I'm serious!"

"Well, I am too and there's no way we're using you for a rabbit. End of discussion."

I wanted to argue but it felt too wonderful having his arms protectively tighten around me, knowing he was concerned for my safety. So I did the next best thing and submitted gracefully.

## Chapter 21

The next morning I woke up to the ringing of my cell phone. Glancing at the caller ID, I saw Alyssa was calling and hastily answered.

"Good morning!" her chipper voice came across, "I hope I didn't wake you! Did I call too early?"

My groggy reassurance gave me away.

"I'm so sorry!  I just wanted to see if it was okay for Erik and me to stop by tomorrow. We'll bring you guys lunch. Also I talked to Howard Angle this morning and he wants to come; is that okay?"

My mind slowly caught up.

"You want to drive up here?"

Alyssa laughed. "Yes! I'm worried about you and want to make sure you really are okay after that accident. But since you got hurt, Erik refuses to let me go alone."

I smiled, her concern warming my heart. "I'd love to see you."

"And Howard?"

*The more the merrier,* I thought. "Of course. Mr. Talcos would love the company."

Alyssa chattered on but my mind zoned out. I was brought back by her saying very clearly through the line, "But of course that's ridiculous, Declan would never suspect Erik of trying to steal from him."

"What?" I asked, suddenly waking up. "I missed that last part."

Alyssa's voice was indignant, "Oh it's nothing. I was just saying that Erik was complaining that Declan never really told him what was going on. He wondered if it was because Declan didn't trust him."

My bleary eyes focused on the far window and I concentrated on what she was saying.

"Did Erik say that Declan didn't trust him with something specific? Or just that he feels that way in general?"

"Oh, no; it's nothing. I'm just venting. Anyway, we'll see you tomorrow. Can't wait!"

She hung up, leaving me wide awake. Time was passing and I didn't feel any closer to figuring out Declan's murder.

Sighing, I rolled off the bed, still sore, and went to prepare for the day.

Mr. Talcos and I spent another quiet morning in the suite. Adam stopped by after dinner, acting like his old self. He announced that they were installing a complete security system at the house and that the press had moved on to other, more exciting stories. By his estimate, he thought we could go home by the end of the week. The fact that there was still a murderer and embezzler on the loose had him worried but he skipped over that little detail rather quickly.

Soon after his arrival, Mr. Talcos kissed me on the cheek affectionately and announced he was heading to bed early. I went into the kitchenette and made two cups of tea before returning to snuggle up with my good shoulder against Adam, who was sitting on the couch. He reached out immediately and put his arm around me, tucking me into his side. I handed him a mug and then rested my head against his arm.

"We're still good?" I asked, uncertainty besieging me.

I felt him sigh, "Still good."

A minute later, as I took a sip of my still hot beverage, I heard Adam chuckle quietly and say, "I don't think he minds."

I looked up at him in surprise, "Who minds what?"

"Your grandfather-in-law. That I'm here." He gave my shoulders a small squeeze and then released me. "That we're here."

I thought about it and realized that Mr. Talcos really did seem okay with my burgeoning relationship with Adam. Following on the heels of my marriage to his grandson, he had every right to suspect or even resent it. Instead, he seemed to not only like Adam, but encouraged us to spend time together.

Settling back in silence, I thought about my strange relationship with Declan. The closer I got to Adam, the more apparent it became to me that although I had respected Declan and trusted him, it was a far cry from loving him.

My mind drifted and I realized I had forgotten to tell Adam about our plans for lunch tomorrow. After explaining the headcount, I asked if he could come. He agreed and I mentally added one more person for our impromptu fiesta. I'd text Alyssa in the morning, just so she knew to bring enough food.

The time flew by and before I knew it, it was eleven o'clock. I stood and tried to hurry Adam. He let me pull him up from the couch and we walked together to the door.

Instead of opening it, he turned and fastened his eyes on mine. I froze.

"Stitches come out tomorrow?" he asked casually, one hand lifting to caress my forehead. I had stopped covering it with a bandage the second day as the thing wouldn't stay in place with my hair in the way. Adam's touch made me shiver and I nodded mutely, taking a step towards him as if drawn towards a magnet.

His hand dropped to his side and then came back up to rest lightly at my waist. Careful of my injured arm, he drew me even closer and the magnetic pull I'd felt before magnified a hundredfold. I held my breath as his other hand came up and settled under my chin.

"Aimee," he said hoarsely, then cleared his throat, "May I kiss you goodnight? Or is it too soon?"

I smiled as butterflies exploded inside. I had never felt like this before in my life. I wanted to say something witty but it was all I could do just to breathe. So I nodded mutely, my cheeks flushing, and waited to see what would happen.

That's all it took and suddenly I was pulled close and his lips were on mine, first gently and then with more pressure until I felt like I couldn't stand any more. Pulling back, I looked up into his darkened eyes, electricity zipping through us and leaving me feeling dazed and I don't know what else.

He looked almost as stunned but regained his composure quickly, a huge grin lighting up his face.

"Wow," he said.

"Wow," I replied, barely breathing.

He pulled me back towards him and I expected another kiss. Instead he enfolded me in a warm hug.

"I should go," he whispered.

Unable to do more than nod as he stepped away and opened the door, I watched him disappear before shutting and locking it. Then I turned and leaned my back against the wall, slowly sliding down until I sat on the floor. My lips tingled and my heart shouted that the most amazing thing in all the world had just happened and it had happened to me.

Covering my face, I wanted to giggle but remembered that I wasn't alone in the suite. Somewhat regaining my composure, I stood up to turn off the lights and then headed to bed. Sleep was a long time coming.

## Chapter 22

The next morning passed in a blur of activity. My stitches came out and then I went to an appointment with an orthopedist for my shoulder. He had me perform a series of painful arm movements and then declared me fine, reassuring me that the pain would lessen and I should have full movement in a matter of weeks. He scheduled me to start physical therapy in ten days. I had been so caught up in the moment, it was strange making plans for the future.

As I conveyed my health insurance information to the receptionist, I wondered if it was still valid. If I was going to step into my role as Declan's widow, then I needed to officially resign from my telemarketer job. Strange but everything from my former life seemed like a distant dream, a life someone else had lived, not me.

Lunch was interesting. Alyssa and Erik brought a huge bouquet of flowers for me. I could tell they felt somewhat responsible for my accident since it had happened after visiting them. Howard also brought a small bouquet, his boisterous hug almost knocking me off my feet. The man was a giant.

After delicious lasagna that Alyssa had prepared herself, we took cups of coffee into the small sitting area. Adam sat next to me on the arm of my chair and I saw Alyssa shoot me a questioning glance, one eyebrow lifted.

I shrugged my good shoulder and smiled at her, a newfound confidence in Adam's and my relationship allowing me to sip my coffee as if it were perfectly normal to have him beside me.

A few minutes later, my phone beeped and I looked down to see a text from her.

"Is there something you want to tell me??!!!" I laughed to myself and shot her a quick message promising I'd tell her later, in private. Adam peered over my shoulder, read our messages and then asked me in a whisper if I wanted him to move. I gave him a look like he was crazy, shook my head no, and then turned my attention back to the group.

Howard was talking about the stock market. Erik was following along and as I watched the two men rehash that morning's reversals, I realized that the three men, including Mr. Talcos, who best knew the company and were closest to Declan were currently in this room.

I was lost in thought when I realized Howard Angle was trying to get my attention. He invited me to step out on the balcony to have a word in private with him and I immediately looked at Adam for permission.

The balcony had been off limits since we'd arrived and I had yet to open the door leading out to it, let alone step outside. Although Adam had mentioned the possibility of returning to the house, the police still hadn't given us the go ahead to leave the room.

I waited until I received a small, almost imperceptible nod from Adam and then turned and accepted Howard's invitation.

I was pleased to find a lovely view of the small beachside town below us with a small strip of ocean visible in the distance. Turning from the charming vista, I faced Howard, curious as to what he had to say.

"My dear," he began, his normally booming voice unusually quiet, "Alfred told me that he informed you about Declan's part in the embezzlement."

I bristled, immediately wanting to deny his statement but he continued unperturbed, "I'm not saying he was guilty, but I want you to know there is a little bit more to the story."

I paused, waiting for him to continue, and then realized he had pulled a chair forward to offer me a seat. Waiting until I was settled, he took the one opposite from me and began to elaborate.

"Declan came to me the day before his disappearance. He was very upset."

"In the afternoon?" I asked, confused. "I thought that appointment was with the three of you: Declan, you and Mr. Talcos."

"You know more than I realize," he said, folding his hands over his ponderous abdomen. "No, there was a meeting scheduled later in the day but I'll get there. Declan came to me in the morning to tell me his USB with all his passcodes and account information was missing. We had already uncovered the fact that the money had been taken through his access codes."

He looked embarrassed as he admitted, "I guess I was suspicious that he was lying. At the time, though, I think we were all suspicious of everybody."

His face cleared. "Anyway, I had told Declan plenty of times he was foolish for putting all his passwords on a USB but I guess Declan thought locking it up in his office safe would keep it protected."

Howard took a deep breath and sighed before continuing, "Declan also told me something the FBI hadn't mentioned. He discovered the paper trail led right to a bank account owned by his grandfather. He thought someone was setting his grandfather up but he didn't know who. He said he had a few more things to look into and then he was going that afternoon to Maine to talk with Alfred. We were going to conference call that night and try to come up with a plan, but they didn't connect online or answer my phone calls. I found out the next day that Declan didn't go to Maine that night and that he never talked to his grandfather."

My mind immediately went to Vicky and her report to the police. Something had happened between that morning when Declan had talked to Howard and later that evening when he'd asked her to book him a ticket out of the country.

Nick Santos. According to Declan's calendar, if he hadn't conference called with Mr. Talcos and Howard, then Nick would have been the last person Declan had a meeting with before he disappeared.

Unfortunately, I remembered from our previous conversation that Nick denied any remembrance of such an encounter.

Pushing aside my musings, I focused on Howard, who suddenly appeared much older than he had only a few moments ago. Reaching out, I patted his arm comfortingly.

"Thank you for telling me about the USB," I told him, trying to convey my appreciation for his honesty. "We both know it wasn't Declan and it wasn't Mr. Talcos. It's just a matter of time before we get to the bottom of this."

Mr. Angle nodded and gruffly replied, "I hope you're right, young lady. I'm kind of hoping the money will just turn up somewhere and we'll know who it is because they have it. But the FBI tells me it isn't likely."

His words echoed my own sentiments from just a few days ago. I sighed, sensing that every piece of information was bringing me closer to the heart of the mystery and at the same time confusing me more.

We returned just in time to say goodbye to Alyssa and Erik. Alyssa pulled me into the hall to walk her to the elevator, and while Erik stood patiently holding the door open with his finger on the button, she gave me a quick shake down.

"Adam? What is going on there?" Expecting censure, I was relieved to see only curiosity and a little excitement reflected in her face.

"It's a long story," I told her, lowering my voice even though only Erik was in earshot.

"Something happened in the hospital between us and I'm not even sure what it means. He took himself off the case because, as he put it, it's a conflict of interest."

I bit my lip, not sure what else to say. Alyssa squeezed my upper arms, smiling.

"He's a good guy, Aimee, but be careful. For crying out loud, you've been a widow for less than a month."

My face flamed and for a moment I felt a fleeting sense of shame. Was I wrong to have feelings for Adam?

Alyssa pulled me into a hug. "Oh honey, just be careful, okay?"

She let me go and joined Erik in the elevator.

"I'll call you!" she yelled just before the doors shut.

I walked back to see Howard Angle opening the door to our suite, Mr. Talcos behind him. I kissed Howard's cheek and said goodbye before returning to the sofas in the living area.

Then it was just Mr. Talcos, Adam and me. I thought about telling both of them about Howard's story but after deliberating between upsetting Mr. Talcos or just letting things go, I decided to tell Adam in private. I honestly didn't know if Mr. Talcos was aware his own account had been used in the heist or if he knew about the USB.

Unfortunately I never really had more than a moment alone with Adam and he left before our supper was delivered. So later that night, I called him from the privacy of my bedroom.

His first question after I explained was, "So where's the USB now?"

I paused; it was something I hadn't even considered.

"I have no idea."

"It's something to think about. I wonder if the FBI knows of its existence."

"Are you going to tell them?" I asked, not sure what I wanted to hear.

His reply was hesitant. "I'm not sure. Probably."

Nervous to examine what I thought of that, I changed the subject.

"Adam, something else. If Declan didn't meet or talk with Howard or Mr. Talcos, then Nick is the last appointment he held that day."

"That could be significant," he said.

"The problem is Nick denied having an appointment."

"He did?" Adam's voice was surprised, "When?"

My cheeks warmed. "I asked him about it when we had coffee together."

I wracked my brain, trying to think of a way to make Nick tell us what had transpired that day. Adam wanted to turn the information over to the police and let them interview him but I was confident that Nick wouldn't answer their questions any more than he did mine.

Then I remembered the secretary.

"Do you think Vickie would remember if Nick came to the office to see Declan?" I asked, feeling a little hope.

"Possibly," Adam answered slowly. "I imagine that day is pretty much imprinted in her memory. And she should have seen them together if they did meet."

"If Vickie can confirm he was there, it might put pressure on Nick to open up," I said, following my train of thought.

"I'll talk to her," Adam said firmly, his tone preventing me from pushing too hard.

"Really?" I asked, surprised he wanted to get involved. "What if she doesn't want to talk to you?"

He chuckled, "Then you can try."

I glanced at the clock; it was after eleven. After briefly exchanging goodnights, I hung up, not quite satisfied but willing to wait.

The next morning, Adam showed up after breakfast with the news that Vickie could indeed confirm Nick's appointment with Declan.

"She seemed hesitant to talk to me at first," Adam recounted, "but when I asked her directly if Declan had met with anyone the evening of his disappearance, she told me that Nick Santos had an appointment. She also said that she saw him leaving the office minutes before Declan called her in and requested her aid with the flight reservations."

"Why didn't she say something sooner?" I asked, walking over to where he stood in the kitchenette pouring a cup of coffee for himself. I passed him my empty mug and he turned to refill it.

"She said she didn't think about it at the time. I don't know. I just hope she's not holding anything else back. It seems every time we turn around, we find something else that someone is covering up."

I knew what he meant. All the things that I had discovered were things that had to be excavated with a pick and brush.

Shrugging my shoulders, I accepted the cup of coffee he held out and led the way back to the sitting room. I glanced out the window at the silhouette of Mr. Talcos on the balcony, glad he was finally able to get a little fresh air. Then I settled onto the sofa.

"I guess the next step is to go in and talk to Nick Santos," I said, making myself comfortable on the couch.

"You mean have the police talk to Nick."

Adam sat down beside me. One hand held his coffee and the other came to rest comfortably on my knee.

I made a face at him. "Do you think he'll really talk to them?"

He grunted, lifting his drink to take a sip. We sat in contemplative silence until I broke it.

"It just seems wrong to suspect Nick," I told him, leaning my head against his shoulder, "because if he was guilty, wouldn't he just take the money and leave the country? Why stick around?"

Adam nodded and we grew quiet again.

My ideas were mostly about how I could convince Adam to let us talk directly with Nick. I knew he adamantly opposed the idea of getting involved or going around the police and FBI, but we needed answers and there was always the possibility that we would find something the police weren't looking for.

My cup was empty again when I eventually came out and just asked if we could drive to Boston and talk to Nick. As expected Adam vehemently objected, putting down his empty cup and using his hands to emphasize the multiple reasons why it wasn't a good idea for us to go. He even brought up my recent accident, pointing out how dangerous it could be for me to visit Boston.

He ended his argument with, "Aimee, this is an ongoing investigation. We can't interfere with that."

I looked at him in exasperation. He was such a rule-follower. "We're not interfering! We're just talking to an old friend of Declan's. It's not like we are forcing him to tell us anything. And you don't have an official capacity in this case, so it's not being unprofessional."

Adam's gaze intensified, "I don't want you involved more than you already are."

I wanted to scoff but at the same time I recognized that his desire to protect me was more than just male dominance or some chauvinistic trait. He cared about me.

I tried to compromise.

"Then you talk to him. I'll just drive into Boston with you. It's not like I need to sit in on the conversation. I could visit Alyssa and Eric, maybe try to talk to Vickie again."

I had told him that Alyssa thought there was something Vickie was hiding and with all the excitement of the car accident, I still hadn't talked to her.

"It's not safe. And you're supposed to stay in the safe house," Adam was not giving in.

"But I'll be with you," I coaxed, hoping to change his mind. "Don't you think I'll be safer where ever you are rather than staying here waiting for your return?"

He tried to cover it, but his smirk as I begged told me I was wearing on him.

"We'd have to get permission from Irons."

"Okay," I said, realizing I had him almost convinced. "And remember, I've already talked to Nick about that meeting. If anything, it might jog his memory to see me before you two discuss it."

His eyebrow quirked and he grinned. "That's reaching. Didn't you just tell me he didn't remember the appointment?"

I shrugged like that bit of information was irrelevant.

His smile turned into full-fledged laughter and he put his arm around me, drawing me close. I shut my eyes as he tucked my head under his chin and I felt my insides melting.

We were silent as we sat, peace slowly filling me. Then I pulled back and looked up, not ready to give in until he let me go with him.

His telling gaze met mine and I knew he was weakening.

"I shouldn't let you come. It's not safe."

I didn't say anything as he continued, "If we had any reason to think this guy was walking around Boston with three million dollars in his wallet, I wouldn't let you."

I bit back a grin. He was talking himself into letting me go. "But as you say, why would he still be in the country if that were the case?"

My arm gave me a little twinge so I shifted my weight, repositioning my injured shoulder.

"We'll go today?" I asked, knowing the answer already.

His gaze hovered around my mouth before meeting my eyes.

"Maybe in a little while?" he asked boyishly, making me grin.

I laughed and gave him a light peck before standing up.

"I'll go get ready. We can pick up from here later on."

His hand caught my good arm as I moved away from the couch and I looked back at him.

"Promise?" Adam asked, the intensity of his dark blue eyes causing my heart to beat erratically. I swallowed and nodded, scared of the feelings suddenly conjured up by just one look. I hastily pulled free and hurried to my room, aware that he was watching me each step of the way.

## Chapter 23

Adam let Detective Irons know we were heading to Boston but didn't say exactly why. After a quick stop to fuel up in town, we merged onto the highway heading south. We rehashed what we knew about the case and though that didn't shed any new light, it did make the time pass quickly.

About half way there, I had a thought. What if Nick wasn't in his office? Then we would be driving all the way to Boston for nothing.

"Why don't I call and make sure he's really there? I can just ask his secretary."

Adam reached into his pocket and handed me his phone. "Use mine, the number is blocked and won't show up on caller ID."

I turned it on and a smiling golden retriever greeted me.

"You have a dog?"

Adam smiled. "Betsy. She's six. I'll have to introduce you to her."

I swiped open the front screen and found the phone app.

"Should I just call the main number for Autem?"

"Yeah, it should be saved under recents."

I quickly found it and pressed call.

"Hello, Autem Viris Bioresearch and Pharmaceutical Company. This is Vickie. How can I direct your call?"

I froze as I recognized Declan's secretary speaking, remembering how she had disappeared on my last visit and never called me back after I left her that sticky note message. Did I want her to know I was tracking down Nick or on my way to Boston? Not if I was going to talk to her too.

Then my telemarketer skills came into play.

"Vickie?" I said in a peppy voice, "yes, my name is Olivia and I'm calling for Nick Santos. Is he in the office?"

Adam raised an eyebrow at my obvious fib and falsely chipper voice.

"I think so. I can transfer you to his secretary."

The call waiting clicked on and I was subjected to several minutes of a violin and piano concerto before someone picked up.

"Nick Santos' office; how may I help you?"

It was the voice of an older woman and I decided it was easier to just continue the charade.

Putting an extra ounce of pep into my voice, I said "Yes, this is Olivia. I'm calling from Starza Mobile with a great offer. For only thirty dollars a month, Mr. Santos can have unlimited wifi access, all the long-distance he wants during non-peak hours and for a special, unlimited time we will throw in 24 accumulatory hours of free calling during peak. Is Mr. Santos in his office today?"

There was a pause.

"Mr. Santos is here but unfortunately occupied. I will tell him you called."

There was a click and the woman hung up the phone. I turned off Adam's cell and handed it back to him.

"Nick's there."

He took it without saying a word, his eyes never leaving the road. The silence stretched out and became uncomfortable.

"Everything okay?" I asked, noting a frown as he concentrated on the inner city traffic.

Adam nodded but then the corners of his mouth dipped further. I tried to figure out what was bothering him and then it hit me.

"You don't like that I was faking on the phone, do you?" I asked, sudden understanding making me annoyed and slightly ashamed.

He hesitated. "It's partly that, partly that you did it so easily."

He slowed to a stop at a red light and I took that opportunity to defend myself, "It wasn't that it was easy for me. My name is Olivia, Aimee Olivia, and I just gave them the spiel I use every day of the week when I make phone calls for work."

I bit my lip waiting for his reaction. I was surprised to see something akin to relief cross his face and for a moment a cold vise tightened on my heart. Did Adam still wonder if he could trust me?

We arrived at the parking garage a little while later and drove around for nearly ten minutes before finding a space. After we parked, I climbed out my side and walked toward the stairs, waiting a few car lengths away for Adam to lock the door.

He came around to join me and I heard him say something. His words were lost though because in that moment I spotted the very person we were there to see, climbing into his black, four-door sedan on the opposite side of the garage.

Nick's eyes connected with mine and then did a double take, obviously recognizing me. I don't know whether his initial reaction was to run away, but I definitely saw him picking up speed as I raced towards his car, Adam close behind.

Since I was yelling and knocking on the windows before he even had the engine on, Nick had little choice but to roll down his window and acknowledge we were there.

With a sigh that was definitely not welcoming, he climbed back out and faced us, the door a barrier between us with his hand on the inside handle.

"Mrs. Talcos," he said, his smile coming across as a grimace, "so nice to see you again. Is there something I can do for you?"

At this point, Adam stepped past me and placed a hand on top of the door, effectively keeping Nick from shutting it.

"We were really hoping you had time to talk," Adam said in what I was beginning to recognize as his no-nonsense, cop voice. I saw his knuckles tighten.

Nick glanced at me and then back at Adam, cautiously leaning away before inquiring, "And who are you?"

One-handed, Adam reached in his back pocket and pulled out a small ID case I'd never seen before. Flipping it open, he introduced himself as Detective Adam Harrison.

Nick looked unimpressed.

Adam's face hardened. "This isn't a formal call, but I have a few questions for you in regards to Declan Talcos' murder. It won't take more than half an hour and it would be completely voluntary on your part."

Nick looked contemptuous for an instant before schooling his features.

"Completely voluntary?" he asked guardedly. "I guess I can chat for a few minutes. Where do you want to talk?"

His compliance was unexpected and I glanced at Adam in surprise.

"Why don't we grab a cup of coffee?" asked Adam, not showing any reaction. He released the door.

It swung immediately towards Nick and I realized that an unseen tug of war had been going on, making me aware of an undercurrent between the two men I hadn't sensed before.

We waited for Nick to grab his wallet from the center console of his car. As he straightened back up, I noticed his badge attached to his lapel, Declan's company logo imprinted underneath his name.

"Do you work for Autem Viris? I thought you ran your own private company."

Nick bristled, "I work for myself; the badge is for access. Since I contract through Autem, my badge has their name on it."

He walked around to pop the trunk, stowing his briefcase inside. His voice came from behind the lifted hatch, "I've contracted with that company for fourteen years. I have access to pretty much everything."

He shut the lid and then our eyes met. His gaze was defiant as it held mine. I felt the need to apologize but I wasn't sure why. Instead I bit my lip and watched Nick gesture with his hand towards the stairwell.

I followed the two men out of the garage, wondering if Adam would notice I was tagging along and ask me to leave. We walked up the street to the skyscraper that housed Declan's bioresearch firm and then went down to the basement café where Nick and I had shared our first cup of coffee.

It was only when the elevator touched ground that Adam turned and asked if I was going to check in with Alyssa. As much as I wanted to stay for their conversation, I knew I had to keep my word to Adam. Nodding, I reached out to push the button for her floor when Nick stopped me by lightly pulling my hand back.

"It might be easier to talk with the three of us. After all, this is about Aimee's husband." He squeezed and then slowly released my fingers. Instead of feeling grateful he wanted to include me, his touch left me with the irrational desire to run away.

Adam stepped closer to me and we entered the café.

There wasn't a line this time and after placing our orders, we found a table, close enough to hear when our coffees were called but not close enough for the laughing baristas to overhear our conversation.

Adam skipped the small talk and got right to business, "I just need to check a few facts, Nick. It's okay if I call you Nick, isn't it?"

He didn't wait for a response, but dove right in. "Where were you on the morning of Declan's murder?"

Nick looked fleetingly surprised at the abrupt nature of the question and then sat back smugly.

"What day was that exactly?" he asked.

Adam gave him the date and I watched as Nick pretended to think.

"I must have been working," he said after a miniscule pause. "I usually am in the morning on a weekday. I know I wasn't in Maine, if that's what you're suggesting."

His eyes grew cold. "And my secretary can attest to my whereabouts."

I glanced at Adam and could tell we thought the same thing; Nick's answer was just a little too vague and a little too pat. I knew Adam would be following up on his alibi.

Adam continued with his line of questioning, "Aimee tells me she talked to you about a meeting you had with Declan the evening before he disappeared. At the time you mentioned you couldn't remember if you met with him. It appears that Declan's secretary doesn't have the same problem and remembers specifically seeing you leave his office on the afternoon in question. Do you think you can remember any more about that meeting?"

Adam's voice took on an almost derisive quality, which surprised me. "Think, Nick, it would have been the last time you saw Declan."

Nick stared openly at Adam, an almost trapped look appearing on his face before he was in control again. The mask that dropped down exuded confidence and unconcern.

He picked up his coffee and swirled it around before asking sarcastically, "Does she say anything else? Was she listening in on our conversation too?"

Adam's expression was pointed, "So you do remember the meeting now."

Nick sighed and put down his cup. "Yes, of course I remember."

He glanced at me, looking strangely apologetic. Then with a big sigh, he explained, "I didn't want to tell Aimee because what we talked about were the suspicions Declan had of his grandfather. He showed me how his accounts had been hacked with his own passwords and the money transferred to his grandfather's account. He wanted my opinion, as a family friend, how to approach his grandfather about this."

At the same time I heard the words, I had trouble believing them. This whole time I had been under the impression that Declan assumed his grandfather was set up. For me, that had been confirmed yesterday by Howard Angle's confession. Nick telling us Declan suspected his grandfather just didn't jive.

"What did you think about what he told you?" I asked, ready to refute his claim that Declan believed his grandfather was the embezzler.

Nick hesitated and then smoothed it over with, "I wasn't completely surprised. Alfred had been coming to the office more frequently as of late and a couple of times I saw him coming out of Declan's office without any sign of Declan in it."

"Did Declan say anything about something of his being stolen?" interjected Adam.

I raised my eyebrows in silent inquiry, wondering why he was hinting about the USB, but Nick readily answered.

"He might have insinuated it. Nothing specific." His eyes narrowed. "Is something missing?"

My attention was distracted by the barista hollering our names in an increasingly loud, nasally voice. From her annoyed expression, I wondered how long she had been calling for us.

Not appreciating the interruption, I jumped up and brought all three coffees over to the table. Adam thanked me with a smile and Nick nodded, taking his coffee and dumping three packs of sugar into it. I handed him a stirrer. From our interaction so far, I wondered if a few more packets might be in order.

Before I could suggest it, Adam asked another question. "Was there ever a time you saw Mr. Talcos, senior, in the office alone with the safe open?"

I unexpectedly had to cover a smile. He sounded like a detective, on duty or not.

Nick sipped his coffee, effectually buying himself time to answer before replying, "A couple weeks ago I knocked on Declan's office door; I think it was just a few days before he left. I know news of the embezzlement had already broken to the media and we had FBI all over. I found Mr. Talcos alone in Declan's office, hastily closing the door to the safe as I walked in."

Suspicious, I offered a question, "What were you doing going into Declan's office unannounced?"

Nick frowned. "Declan and I have been friends for almost three decades. I usually gave a courtesy knock and just entered."

His declaration surprised me. Clarifying his statement, I asked him, "Three decades? Didn't you and Declan meet in college?"

His expression was indecipherable as he said, "We met back up in college but we knew each other when we were kids."

He put so much effort into not showing emotion as he said this that I got the impression he was hiding much stronger feelings. I left it alone.

Adam broke in, his own thoughts obviously going down a different track, "Have you mentioned this to the FBI?"

Nick looked at us speculatively, as if judging what our reaction would be. "No, I didn't want to tell the FBI because I didn't want to get the old man in trouble. After all, he built this company from the ground up. If he needed money from it," he shrugged, "I guess it was his to take."

I frowned, not buying his explanation.

Adam seemed skeptical too.

"So you thought Mr. Talcos was stealing from the company, but failed to tell any one."

His eyes burned. "No, I didn't know who it was. That's what Declan thought."

"Did you tell Declan that you had seen his grandfather in his office?" Adam asked.

Nick nodded. "I didn't think it right to keep it from him."

"So why did you think it was okay to keep it from the police after Declan was found murdered, with his grandfather there, in his grandfather's home?"

Nick winced, not answering, and not looking at us.

I glanced at Adam. What was he getting at? It wasn't common knowledge that Mr. Talcos had an alibi for the morning of the murder. Was he trying to get Nick to admit he thought Declan was murdered by his own grandfather?

His cop visage in place, Adam pressed, "What did you think when you heard Declan was found shot?"

Nick paled but answered, "By that point I felt it would confuse things more if I told what I had seen. And honestly, I had kept quiet for so long I worried that it might get me in trouble for not saying something in the first place. It seemed easier to not get involved."

"So you would rather someone get away with Declan's murder than inconvenience yourself?"

Adam's question was brutal and Nick took the direct hit. His eyes lit with anger before he replied scornfully, "Declan was always a little full of himself. If someone killed him, it was probably no more than he deserved."

This statement made my blood boil. The man's arrogance was driving me crazy and it must have been apparent on my face. Adam squeezed my knee under the table warningly and I tried to calm down.

"I thought you were friends," I finally said as dozens of other less kind accusations ran through my mind.

Nick's eyes were dark and cold as he told me, "You can know someone a long time and never really be friends."

I shivered at the look in his eyes and Adam chose that moment to end our interview.

"Well, thank you for your help," Adam said, squeezing my knee one more time before removing his fingers and reaching across the table to shake Nick's hand. "We appreciate your time and answering our questions. If you don't mind, I'd like to get your number in case I have anything more to ask you."

I picked up our empty cups and disposed of them while Adam programmed Nick's number into his phone.

I joined them by the entranceway and Nick's eyes met mine.

"I hope you can get to the bottom of this without anyone getting hurt." His comment was amiable but it made me squirm uncomfortably. "I mean anyone else." He was still looking at me.

I went to pass him and then stopped, one more question on my tongue.

"Nick," I said, curious what he would say. "Mr. Talcos told me you were once engaged to Elyse. Why did she break up with you?"

Nick swallowed, my question obviously taking him by surprise. He licked his lips before answering, "She fell in love with another man. I wasn't good enough for her anymore."

I felt Adam step up close behind and place a hand on the small of my back. He asked directly, "Are you sure you didn't have something to do with it?"

I realized he was thinking of what Elyse had said about the letter Nick had written.

Nick shook his head and I saw banked fires as he lifted his eyes to focus on Adam. "She was used to having whatever she wanted. After she had her fun with me, she moved on."

I shivered involuntarily at the resentment I saw buried within his explanation. Adam gently pulled me away by tugging on my elbow and I turned to follow.

"Do you want to check in with Alyssa or Vickie before we head back?" he asked, once we were out of Nick's hearing.

As much as I wanted to talk about what we had just heard, I agreed we should try to talk to both of them. Unfortunately neither Erik nor Alyssa were in the building and Vickie was extremely busy. We waited for a good half hour but there was a constant influx of people into the office and so we never had the opportunity to ask her anything privately.

Vickie did say one thing as we made our adieus. Giving me a warm hug, she whispered in my ear that she was sorry she had been so quick to call the authorities and that she had regretted it ever since. That made me feel a little better and I found myself liking her much more than the first time I had met her.

We arrived back at the hotel shortly before four. Adam brought me to the door of our suite, kissed my cheek chastely, and told me he'd return later. He asked me to keep mum about our interview with Nick for now and I agreed.

I presumed Adam was talking to Detective Irons and maybe asking him to check up a little on Nick. We had gone over what we had learned on the way home and we both felt that the oddest part of the story, besides Nick's reason for the break up between him and Elyse, was Declan talking to him about his grandfather stealing money but then not telling him about the missing USB.

I released a deep breath after Adam left, remembering the promise I had made to him just that morning that we would continue where we had left off. Part of me had hoped he would forget but now a bigger part of me was disappointed that he had.

I thought of his hand warmly squeezing my knee in the café earlier and blushed. Our relationship was proceeding rapidly, so fast that I was scared I couldn't keep up. I hesitated to admit it, but it was true. I might have been married and spent twenty-four years living in this world but when it came to boyfriends and real relationships, I was still a sweet sixteen.

To distract myself, I tried to focus on the case. I thought back to the reason Nick had given for the demise of his engagement. It obviously wasn't the same excuse Elyse had given Adam, but had Elyse actually told Nick the real reason she was breaking up with him? Or had she told him she had met someone else in order to save face?

Reasoning aside, Nick harbored a considerable amount of resentment toward Elyse. Eight years seemed a long time to carry a grudge, especially when the person who injured you had been dead for the last five.

## Chapter 24

Detective Irons came the next day with good news and bad news.

The good news, we could return home. Security systems had been installed and the police were planning on driving by to make spot checks. Hearing we could return lifted my spirits. As nice as the hotel suite was, I missed the sound of the ocean and drinking coffee out back in the morning.

The bad news, unfortunately, was that the FBI had concluded their investigation of the embezzlement and it looked like they were going to impugn Declan.

Adam's news was disappointing too. He told me privately that Nick's secretary had confirmed Nick was at work the morning of Declan's murder.

Speaking of secretaries, I had an unexpected phone call while the detective was over. Looking at my caller ID, I saw a Boston area code. I excused myself and went to the balcony to take the call. Declan's former secretary was at the other end.

"Aimee? It's Vickie." Her voice was devoid of emotion, making me wary.

"Yes, how are you?"

She let go of a sigh, sounding impatient. "I have your number from when you left it on my desk. I know I never called you back and when you stopped by last time, I basically avoided you."

She had seemed busy the last time we tried to talk to her, but I hadn't realized it was deliberate.

"Why are you calling me now?" I didn't want to be rude, but I was confused. And even though she had instigated this conversation, I felt like she was annoyed that she had to talk to me.

"I'm leaving for California this evening. I'm not going to see you again. I wanted to apologize for what happened."

Her voice sounded anything but apologetic.

"It's okay," I said anyway. "It wasn't your fault."

There was a pause.

"There's something else. I don't even want to tell you, but I have to get this off my conscience before I take off to start a new life."

I waited, my heart suddenly pounding at what she was saying.

"Declan never asked me to book a flight to Central America. I called the police after eavesdropping on his and Nick Santos' conversation and heard Nick tell Declan that he knew about his grandfather. After Nick left, I went into Declan's office. He was going through papers, his back to me, and I heard him mutter something about leaving."

I felt my anger flare. "So you made a story up about him so you wouldn't have to admit you were spying?"

For the first time her attitude diminished. "I made up the story because I didn't want to admit I was trying to blackmail him."

"You were what?" I said astonished; what was she saying?

"I told him I'd report his grandfather to the police if he didn't give me ten thousand dollars."

I was too surprised to say anything.

"Aimee," her bravado was completely gone, "he told me I didn't know what I was talking about, that he was more guilty than his grandfather, and that he was leaving. I was angry, but he was right. I didn't hear everything he and Nick had discussed and I didn't know what I was talking about. So I called the police and told them he was escaping. When they questioned me how I knew, it seemed safer to tell them a fib than the truth."

I didn't know what to say. Vickie's story validated Nick's claims that Declan had suspected his grandfather. The fact that Declan had run away made him seem guilty. Nothing was coming together in my mind.

Thankfully Vickie was ready to hang up once she made her confession. After thanking her for the information, I ended the call and then went to look for Adam.

He was with Mr. Talcos, the front door just closing behind someone.

"Detective Irons just left," he informed me, then took in my serious countenance.

"Everything okay?"

I nodded but then shrugged. Mr. Talcos was heading towards his room.

"Can we talk outside?" I asked.

Adam came forward, taking my hand and leading me out to the balcony.

From up above we could see Detective Irons climbing in his car. I watched him drive away before turning to face Adam.

"That was Vickie. I've just learned something very interesting."

I told him what Vickie had done and, like me, he was surprised. Then we discussed Declan's actions following her threat, more puzzled by them than before.

"Should we tell anyone?" I asked, as we went back inside the suite. Mr. Talcos had gone into his room.

"You mean like the FBI?" asked Adam. "I can let them know, but I doubt she would admit anything to them."

I realized he was right. Vickie might feel better making a clean breast of it but what she'd told me in private, she would most likely deny if questioned.

"I guess we know the real reason why Declan left and that's what's important. He knew that with Vickie going to the police he would most likely be arrested."

We stood for a bit longer but then Adam had to go. He had family obligations and as much as our relationship had progressed, I wasn't ready to meet his folks.

Mr. Talcos and I shared a quiet meal and then happily packed our bags to ready our selves for the morrow. I texted Alyssa to let her know of our impending release and, unusual though it was, I found myself in my pajamas and asleep by nine.

I was woken up by a text from Adam around eleven. He simply asked if I was awake and free to chat. Sending back one word *yes*, my phone immediately began to ring.

Trying to sound more alert than I was, I attempted a cheerful, "Hey! How's it going?"

I must not have pulled it off very well because Adam called me on it straightaway.

"You were sleeping!" he accused.

"Well, I had to wake up in order to read your text!"

"You should have ignored it," he said, but I could hear the amusement in his voice.

"It's not like I was going to be able to go back to bed wondering what you wanted," I replied, stifling a yawn.

He laughed and lowered his voice slightly, "Besides wanting to tell the most beautiful woman in the world goodnight, I also wanted to tell her that I asked Detective Irons to check up on Nick."

I smiled to myself, knowing he was teasing and liking it all the same.

"What did he find out?" I asked, more awake.

"His background check is interesting. He grew up in a rather poor family. Apparently he was put into foster care and then returned to his dad several times before he was seven. He filed for emancipation from his father, whom he was living with, when he was sixteen. The courts granted it to him when he was seventeen. Then he met up with Declan when they were in college."

"Except we know he met Declan when they were much younger," I interrupted, remembering what Nick had said earlier that afternoon."

"Right," Adam said, and I could hear him shuffling papers. "There's no record of that here. Anyway, it appears he started dating Elyse in his mid-twenties after he won several contracts from Declan's company. She was six years younger than him."

"She was older than you?" I asked curiously, instantly doing the math.

"By one year," he answered defensively and I laughed.

"Go on," I encouraged after a pause.

Adam resumed, "Nick's company also subcontracts for the government and he has a pretty decent security clearance."

"Does he employ anyone?" I asked. "I thought he worked out of Autem Viris."

"He has a secretary on his payroll. She takes care of his schedule and typing."

"Anything else unusual?" I asked.

"As far as I could see there was nothing suspicious on his record except for one blip when he was fourteen."

I waited but he didn't continue. "What was that for?"

I heard him rearranging his papers again before he answered, "It says here that he was tried and acquitted for robbery. He was one of four teens arrested after a bank in town was held up. They were all cleared."

"That's strange," I said, not sure what to think of a kid being involved in a bank robbery.

"Well, the odd thing is that he was able to afford lawyers two years later when he applied to be emancipated from his parent," he replied.

Adam was right, that was unusual, but not as incredible as a fourteen year old bank robber.

"So you think at the age of fourteen he was involved in the robbery, somehow made off with the money and then successfully hid it in a place where he could still access it two years later?" I summed up, unable to hide the incredulousness from my voice.

He laughed, "Well, when you say it like that it seems rather impossible to imagine a fourteen year old kid pulling it off."

"Not if he was working with someone," I said, playing devils advocate, "and he got a cut of the money."

"It's possible," Adam admitted but I could tell he thought our theory was rather far-fetched. "The other three were acquitted too. I asked Irons to run their names through the system just for laughs and it seems that all three have ended up spending some time in jail since then."

"So not the best people for him to have hung out with," I murmured.

There was silence on his end of the phone.

"Adam," I said, rolling onto my back and staring up into the darkness, "the idea of someone stealing three billion dollars without leaving a trail seems ludicrous too. We probably can't rule anything out at this point."

Adam agreed and then, completely off-topic, said, "I miss you."

His voice was gentle like a caress and I felt my body temperature rise in response to his tenderness.

"I miss you too," I told him, kicking the covers off my suddenly over-heated feet.

"You're smiling," he laughed and I realized I was.

"You seem to have that effect on me," I teased, realizing how much easier it was to say some things in the dark. "Just thinking of you makes me happy."

"Good," he said, his voice slightly husky before he cleared it. "Keep that thought and I'll see you in the morning."

Just before Adam hung up, I asked him, "Adam?"

"Yah?"

"We'll ask Mr. Talcos about the USB and what Nick said tomorrow, right?"

He was quick to respond, "Yes, but together. I'll be over for breakfast."

I agreed and we said our goodnights. I lay in bed thinking how different my life had become in just a couple weeks before my heavy lids closed and I drifted off to sleep.

## Chapter 25

I woke up early and walked out to find Mr. Talcos sitting in the living area, watching television. I fixed us each a cup of coffee and we sipped while we watched the morning news.

Sure enough, the report of Declan's death had been pushed to the backburner and nothing even related to the embezzlement flashed across the screen.

Finishing quickly, I returned to my room to finish packing.

By eight o'clock, Adam had arrived and the three of us sat down to our last meal together in the hotel suite.

I found it difficult to eat because I was almost sick with apprehension, antsy to go home but even more uptight waiting to find out what Mr. Talcos would say about Nick's accusations yesterday.

Adam looked calm and Mr. Talcos was completely focused on his meal. I wanted to scream at how composed they were.

Finally, pushing his plate back with a contented sigh, Adam tipped his chair back like he had all the time in the world. I shot him a dirty look and he returned it with a wink. Rolling my eyes, I reached over for his plate and took it into the kitchenette along with mine.

Making a second trip for the rest of the dishes, I heard Adam ask Mr. Talcos, "Do you think we could finish our coffee in the living room?"

Quietly scraping off the half eaten food from my plate into the garbage can, I hurried to set it in the sink with the other dishes. I found myself straining to hear their trivial conversation while I turned on the faucet. I knew Adam wouldn't say anything important without me there, but I didn't want to miss a thing.

Washing the dishes in record time, I scooped up my mug of cold coffee from the table and joined Adam on the couch. His arm came around me naturally and I inched closer to his side.

"We met with Nick Santos yesterday," Adam began, looking at the elderly gentleman sitting across from us in a matching chair. "He said some interesting things."

Mr. Talcos nodded his head towards me. "Yes, Aimee told me."

I looked up at Adam with wide eyes. "I told him we saw him, but I didn't tell him any interesting things."

Adam chuckled and his eyes twinkled at my defensive tone. His gaze returned to Mr. Talcos and he began to gently describe our visit and the conversation from yesterday, not making accusations or substantiating Nick's assertions but rather asking for an explanation. He also failed to mention Nick's claim that Declan thought Mr. Talcos was embezzling.

Mr. Talcos took it rather calmly, not interrupting Adam's monologue. His expression was slightly regretful and I realized that while not surprised at what Nick had said regarding his involvement, it still saddened him.

When Adam finished, I was practically holding my breath, gripping his left hand tightly with both of mine. He squeezed and I relaxed my grasp, still maintaining contact.

My grandfather-in-law seemed to be thinking about what Adam had said. His grey-green eyes were unfocused and it occurred to me that as much as I liked and respected this man, I didn't know him very well.

Suddenly, as if coming out of a trance, Mr. Talcos started to speak.

"Elyse fell in love with Nick the moment she met him, when she was very young. He was dark, mysterious and came from a difficult life. As adults, the fact that he worked his way up to be a very successful programmer impressed her. She was sweet but she was spoiled. Tragedy robbed her of her parents, but there wasn't anything else in the world that she couldn't have, just for the asking."

I glanced at Adam, wondering where this was going and what Elyse had to do with our recent conversation about Nick, but I held my tongue.

Mr. Talcos went on, "Nick became a puzzle to her. Sometimes he would be open and accepting and other times he would rebuff her and tease her, not exactly maliciously but rather inconsiderately. I worried about the two of them but I was her grandfather, not exactly her confidant."

He paused and gave a heartfelt sigh. I sensed he thought that he had let her down. This was followed by a cough and we waited for his wheezing to subside.

"She finally came to me one day, telling me they were engaged. It bothered me, because Nick was pressuring her for an elopement. I told her that if he really loved her, he would marry her in the sight of all. She must have taken that to heart because the next thing I knew Nick was in my office, petitioning me for her hand in marriage."

Mr. Talcos met my eyes with obvious regret. "I was still working back then, too much if you asked Declan, and I agreed to the wedding because that was what Elyse wanted. It was one more thing I could give her and I forgot to ask myself if it was best for her. After the engagement, Nick started spending a lot of time with the family. And while showering plenty of physical affection on her, he was also critical of her, even in front of her family and friends; to the point that she was frequently embarrassed."

Mr. Talcos' eyes filled with pain. "This bothered me and I asked Declan if I should get involved. He told me I should let them figure it out and so I took his advice. After all, I had never tried to stop her or change her mind before."

Listening to the tired voice tell of his own fears and failings, my heart filled with sorrow. He had tried so hard to understand and support a young woman at a time when what she probably needed most was a mother. I almost wished I had been there to help her but then realized I would have been a teenager at the time of her engagement.

Unaware of my thoughts, Mr. Talcos continued, "Their wedding was arranged for the following year, the same month that I was planning to retire. I'll admit, my mind was distracted trying to get things in order so that I could step down and I didn't give Elyse the attention I should have."

His eyes closed. "It was less than a month after they set the date that Elyse showed up at my house in Maine. I wasn't living there year round yet, but I was there when she knocked on my front door, bawling her eyes out. She told me about a letter she had accidentally encountered, and then guiltily read, while dropping some things off at Nick's apartment."

"What did it say?" I asked huskily as Mr. Talcos reached up a shaking hand to wipe his brow. I noticed perspiration had broken out across his forehead.

"In it Nick talked about how he was marrying money and how much he was going to enjoy it once they tied the knot. He also said that his intended wasn't very bright and he figured she'd do things his way easily enough."

I looked up at Adam, briefly meeting his eyes. This matched the story he had been told by Elyse, only it was worse, personally attacking her intelligence.

"At first I think she just wanted to pretend she had never read the stupid letter, but after several days she couldn't ignore the fact that the man she loved was marrying her for her money. I told her to break it off with Nick and to stay in Maine until she was over it. She took my advice and remained in the house for the rest of the summer. As far as I know she only saw Nick one more time after that."

"When was that?" Adam asked, breaking into his narrative.

"About a week after she came, Nick finally figured out where she was. He came to the house to speak with her. I came home just as he was leaving. I didn't ask but I imagine she explained to him how she felt. I know he left and as far as I know, never came back."

"How did he take it?" Adam inquired.

"He was angry when he I encountered him, understandably so, but he never gave us any trouble."

"Did you expect him to?"

Mr. Talcos looked thoughtful. "I wouldn't say he was a violent man, but he was definitely quick to let loose an insult. The way he spoke to Elyse, and even Declan, was usually a little condescending."

I knew what he was talking about, remembering our earlier conversation with Nick and his derogatory speech. I wondered why they continued to let him contract with the firm.

"Did this affect his relationship with the company?" Adam inquired, as if reading my mind.

"No, not at all," Mr. Talcos replied, his voice strengthening and sounding confident. "That's business. He excels at what he does and we need his services. It's been a profitable relationship for both of us."

For the first time he spoke with authority and I could see the founder and CEO of a large corporation sitting before me.

He deflated with Adam's next question, "Were you aware Nick saw you in Declan's safe?"

I held my breath, suddenly afraid of the response. He closed his eyes and ran his hand over his face before glancing back and forth between the two of us.

"I remember he came in one time when I was in Declan's office," he said candidly. "I thought I had shut the safe before he entered and that he hadn't noticed it was open."

"But you had opened it?" Adam clarified.

"Yes, maybe three or four weeks ago, a few days before Declan disappeared."

"Why were you in Declan's safe?" Adam asked the obvious question.

Mr. Talcos' pause was so long I thought he wasn't going to answer.

Then he expelled a heavy breath. "There is something I need to tell you, something I should have admitted earlier."

His hands gripped the side arms of his chair and I sat completely still, anticipating his explanation as he collected his thoughts.

Finally he began, "I knew how the money was transferred out before Howard Angle told me. After it was announced we were missing money, I started looking into the accounts on my own. After all, it was my company and I figured if there was something abnormal that needed tracking, I would find it faster than someone who didn't know our system."

His face was drawn and he closed his eyes before saying, "I knew the money left through Declan but I couldn't tell where it went. I thought since it was under his authorization, maybe it went to his account. But I couldn't tell that to the FBI. I also needed to confront Declan."

He opened his eyes and looked directly at Adam. "I wanted to find out if we could put it back with no one the wiser."

"What did you do?" Adam asked, poker face in place.

Mr. Talcos' mouth tilted sheepishly. "I borrowed his USB and made a copy of it. He kept his passwords on it. It wasn't much of a break in. Declan's current office is my old office and he used the same safe with the same code that I had when I was there. At first I thought I could log in from his office computer but after perusing the first account I realized I would need more time to really investigate."

"What did you find?" Adam probed.

"That none of Declan's accounts contained unexplained money."

"When did you put the USB back?" Adam asked.

Mr. Talcos looked away.

"I put it back in the safe the day after Declan was declared missing."

"The day after?" Adam repeated, startled. "Why afterwards?"

Mr. Talcos sighed again and the very old man who I only saw occasionally, emerged. "It was just bad luck that Declan had decided to take off while I still had it. I knew that it would look suspicious to the authorities if they found it on me, especially since I'd managed to trace the money into one of my old work accounts."

His gaze shifted to me. "Imagine my shock when I saw that."

"You weren't worried you'd be caught returning it?" Adam's voice was level and I was impressed at his lack of emotion. I know I felt like crying.

"I had to go into the office anyway," Declan's grandfather explained, "to speak to the investigators. I actually put it back right before they came in and had me open the safe for them to examine the contents."

"Did you know that Declan had discovered the theft?"

Mr. Talcos' voice dropped to a whisper, "No."

"He discovered it that morning."

"That's why he left," he murmured, speaking to himself. "He suspected me."

I took in his defeat and shook my head fiercely. "He might have left, but he didn't think you stole the money."

The last thing I wanted was for Mr. Talcos to believe his grandson thought he was a thief.

"How many people had access to the safe?" asked Adam, drawing Mr. Talcos' attention back to our conversation.

His eyes were hollow and I hurt for him.

"Only Declan and I. However, there are probably plenty of people who could have figured it out. We opened it whenever we needed something, which was pretty frequently, regardless of who was with us."

"Did you destroy the copy of the USB?" Adam shifted forward in his chair.

"No." Mr. Talcos answered.

"Where is it now?" I asked.

Mr. Talcos appeared discomfited as he answered my question. "It was in the safe in my study but it's gone now. I imagine whoever killed Declan took it."

"So whoever killed Declan has access to all of his personal information?" I asked, my voice climbing an octave.

"Not any more," Adam reassured me. "The FBI shut down all his access codes the day after he disappeared."

He turned to Mr. Talcos. "But you knew that, so you didn't say anything."

Mr. Talcos nodded in agreement.

I regarded him thoughtfully. "So we think whoever killed Declan is also the embezzler. That means he would have had all of Declan's information anyway, before he robbed your safe."

I lifted my head to look at Adam still sitting next to me. "Who had access to Mr. Talcos' banking information and also had access to Declan's office?"

"Not exactly my banking information," interposed Mr. Talcos. "It's an old business account, so he really only needed to know the company."

"How well do you know Howard Angle?" I said sharply, my mind jumping to his elderly business partner.

Adam pressed my hand. "Aimee!" he cautioned, "You can't jump to conclusions like that!"

He looked at my grandfather-in-law apologetically, "Sorry, she speaks before thinking sometimes."

I made a face. "I'm sorry! But who else knew how to access the money?"

Adam's eyes warned me to back off and I let it go. We could talk about it later.

Returning to the topic of Declan's murder, I asked another question, "So why did the embezzler come to the house and confront Declan? He already had the money."

"Maybe it wasn't the embezzler," Mr. Talcos offered, apparently not put out by my accusation of Howard.

"There are other theories," Adam mumbled, his voice low. I looked at him and remembered his partnership hypothesis, that Declan had been in on it, turned on his partner and then been stabbed in the back in return.

I narrowed my eyes but didn't say anything, not with Mr. Talcos present.

The gentleman in question cleared his throat uncomfortably, drawing our attention, "I'm not sure how it's related, but there was something else missing from the safe. Something sentimental and not of value to anyone but me."

His eyes clouded with pain and I noticed for the first time a tear on his face. I stood up and walked over, taking his hand in mine and smiling down, encouraging him to continue.

"There was a small box that I kept there for safe keeping. It held my wife's engagement ring, a lock of my son's hair and locks of Declan's and Elyse's hair."

It hit me that after losing a wife, a son and two grandchildren, Mr. Talcos had reached old age only to face it alone.

"I didn't mention it because it really doesn't have any significance for anyone except me."

My grip tightened on his hand and I think he realized I was trying to tell him that I also cared that his treasures had been taken.

"Maybe the thief thought the ring was worth something," I said.

He patted my arm gently with his free hand and then pulled away to wipe away the tear. I looked at Adam with raised eyebrows.

"And you didn't report the USB missing because that might implicate you in the embezzlement." Adam's tone was understanding rather than condemning.

"Yes," Mr. Talcos admitted. "I thought perhaps it was best to say nothing. How could I prove I made the copy after the embezzlement occurred? Naturally the police would assume I made it before in order to use it. I would have placed myself in the uncomfortable position of looking like the embezzler."

A long silence ensued.

"Maybe it's time to head over to the house," I said. I wasn't sure what else to say. Mr. Talcos' admission gave me pause and I found myself even more anxious to find the culprit. It seemed that every person involved had a secret they were hiding. Eventually the pieces had to come together, didn't they?

Both men agreed with my suggestion and Mr. Talcos went to collect his things.

I glanced sideways at Adam, who rose from the couch to stand beside me. Inexplicably, he looked calm. His arm came up to draw me closer, squeezing me gently, careful of my almost recovered shoulder.

"Let's get your stuff," he said above my ear, "we can talk more at the house."

"Okay," I squeaked, resenting how easily he was digesting Mr. Talcos' story.

He let me go and I went into the room that had been my home for the past week. I collected my purse and made sure I had packed my phone charger before joining the men waiting for me in the open doorway.

As I preceded the men out of the suite and towards the elevator, I wondered for the first time if maybe we were being hasty in leaving the hotel so soon. A feeling of unease came over me as I thought of how far away the house was from town and how few of the neighbors were actually home this time of year.

The light from the down button shut off and a bell dinged as the doors slid open. I glanced behind me as I stepped inside, wondering if I should say something to Adam. After all, we were making new discoveries every day. Maybe we should sit tight in the safety of the hotel a little while longer and see if anything else came to light.

I felt silly when I came out into the parking lot and saw the police cars lined up and ready to escort us home. Of course Detective Irons wasn't planning on just dropping us off and running. An officer who looked like he was twelve came up and took Mr. Talcos' suitcase. I turned and saw Adam putting my bag in his trunk. Apparently he was going to drive us home; I found I was perfectly content with that.

## Chapter 26

As we walked up the front stairs to the house, Adam reassured me we would be safe. I hadn't said anything but he seemed to sense my anxiety. Before we went inside, he explained about the new state-of-the-art security system, installed during our absence, and how it would go off if someone broke in, sending police immediately to the house.

I looked into his worried face, his arm around my shoulders, and realized he shared my angst about returning to the house. He stopped explaining for a moment and then pulled me into a hug, resting his chin on my head.

"You don't have to stay here," he murmured. "I can always bring you back to the hotel."

I pulled back and studied his face. "I think you're just nervous because of all that's happened. We'll be fine."

He frowned. "In addition to the security system I'll make sure Irons has a cop drive by and check on you a couple times a day."

I smiled. "Adam, you already told me I couldn't be bait. I really don't think you'd let me return here if it wasn't perfectly safe."

His regard deepened and I felt my heart stop. His gaze fell to my lips and slowly his mouth descended towards mine. I closed my eyes, feeling that things were very right in my world.

We broke apart a moment later to a cacophony of wolf-whistles and I realized the other officers in our caravan were getting quite a show on the front porch. I blushed bright red and stepped back. I noticed Adam's cheeks were pink too and he smiled, shooting me a wink before turning to face his colleagues. Detective Irons was just coming up the stairs.

"Let's do a quick inspection of the house and property. Then we can let these people have some privacy," he ordered.

A voice called out, "We know why they want privacy!" followed by snorts before the men spread out, covering the house and grounds quickly.

I turned back to Adam and held my hands out guiltily.

"Not gonna lie," I said, laughing at him, "I like the idea of privacy too."

Adam chuckled but he stayed where he was, aware that the men still had us in their sights.

The police finished clearing the house and we were able to go inside. Unfortunately Adam had a vet appointment for his dog but promised to come back in the evening.

After he left, I set the alarm as I had been instructed and poked my head into the living room to let Mr. Talcos know it was on. I was glad we had it but it would be a pain since we had to set it every time we opened an outside door.

I carried my bag up to my room and unpacked the few things I owned. The funeral dress was still in the closet. I gazed at it for a moment but then shut the door, not wanting to remember that day.

Then I stood looking out the window. I remembered the last time I'd been there, right before we'd left for the hotel. Once again I let the beauty of the clear sky, grey-blue ocean and bleached sand wash over me. With nary a cloud and the sun shining above, it was hard to believe there were any problems in the world.

That evening a storm blew in. The sea that had seemed so calm just hours before became grey and angry. The wind shook the house and I closed myself off in my room. I knew I should go down and make dinner but I didn't want to leave my nest.

Adam had texted me early on in the afternoon to say he was detained but planned to stop by later in the evening. I wondered hazily if I should find out if he planned to come for supper. Instead I felt my eyes shutting and the world slowly fading away.

Hours later I awoke to a loud thunderclap booming right outside my window. I shivered as I tried to remember where I was. The room was almost pitch black and I was cold. Rolling over, I reached for my bedside table lamp and flicked the switch. Nothing happened.

I pulled myself up with my good arm, the left one still sore with any pushing or pulling movements, and reached down to make sure the cord was still in the outlet. It was.

Pausing another moment to get my bearings, I tried to think where I had left my cell phone. I remembered slipping it back in my purse after my last, short message from Adam, and then I had put my bag on the seat near the window.

Fumbling in the dark, I found the chair and then my purse but no cell phone. At that moment my brain started to function and I realized the bedside clock was also off; meaning we were without power.

Assuming the storm had knocked out the electricity, I felt my way to the door of my bedroom and let myself out. Continuing through the blackened hall with my hand trailing the wall, I found the stairs and made my way down carefully. Straining my eyes through the dark in the direction of the main house, I heard a deep voice coming from the kitchen and made my way towards it.

What I saw when I entered the room caused my stomach to drop. A single candle sat on the counter, it's flickering light illuminating the kitchen bar where Mr. Talcos and Nick Santos sat at opposite ends.

I almost tripped, ready to turn and run, but Nick's mocking voice invited me in.

"I hoped you would join us," he said, his eyes glinting in the candlelight. I caught my breath and I knew innately that I was in danger.

Skirting around the center bar where they sat and sliding to the other side of the kitchen, I put as much of a physical barrier as possible between us. I wished for all the world that I had looked harder for my phone.

Tripping the security alarm for help crossed my mind but I didn't know if that was possible with the power out. Trying not to look like I was scared to death, I leaned back against the opposing counter and stuttered out a reply, "Nick, what are you doing here?"

His grin was malicious and he turned to look at Mr. Talcos. "There were some things I needed to take care of before I leave the country. Some very important things."

I gulped and a cold shudder ran through me. There could only be one reason he was going away. He was the man we were looking for.

In my typical fashion, I blurted out like an idiot, "It was you! You were the embezzler. You killed Declan!"

Everything froze for a second.

Then, instead of denying it, he laughed, the jarring sound sending chills up my spine, "Very good, Aimee. You figured it out."

I felt myself start to shake and realized I needed to get myself in hand. I grabbed onto the handle of the stove beside me and held tight, keeping my knees from buckling.

Mr. Talcos was staring at me with sad eyes full of pain. "I'm so sorry, my dear," he said, his voice cracking with the term of endearment.

"What?" I asked, my breathing starting to accelerate, "You too?"

I felt betrayed, as if part of my heart was being ripped out when Nick's cold voice spoke, "No, not him too."

Nick sat back on the stool and it was only then that I realized he had a gun trained on Mr. Talcos. My respirations slowed and I regained control of myself.

Gripping the handle of the oven, I felt fabric crumple beneath my hand. I looked down and saw a towel. I searched the top of the stove, but not even a pan was nearby.

"Let me tell you a little story," Nick said, his twisted mouth drawing back my attention. "It's about a young boy who was brought into a family for adoption. For almost an entire year he was treated like a prince, given everything he could want or desire, and told he was loved until one day, his biological father returned to claim him."

"Nick," Mr. Talcos broke in, his voice pleading, "We didn't want you to go. There was no way to fight the courts. Your father refused to give up his rights."

Nick looked at his former foster father contemptuously, "You didn't even try. I was only six years old and you fed me back to that lion. Do you know what I went through over the next ten years?" His voice rose and for a moment I saw that little boy wanting to hurt back.

He paused and regained his composure.

"But that's neither here nor there," he continued, his voice once again eerily calm. "That boy was able to rise above his situation. He graduated top of his class and created a great job for himself. He even fell in love."

"You never loved her," Mr. Talcos' voice was low but firm.

"I loved being loved by her," Nick answered roughly. "I loved what she would have given me. But I was never good enough for you, for her, for any of you."

Nick's eyes narrowed. "You talked her out of marrying me."

I realized he was talking about Elyse and wondered, not for the first time, if she had ever told him about the letter she had discovered. I also wondered if I could reach a knife in time to do something with it before I was shot.

"I hated both of you after that, even Declan with his too perfect sympathy. He didn't really care, he couldn't. He never knew what it was like to finally have what you want and then lose it all over again."

Nick's voice rose angrily, "So I determined to do something about it. I was tired of watching you all live your perfect lives and leave me to trudge along behind. Elyse was the first to learn."

My eyes widened and I forgot all about looking for something to defend myself. I stared at Nick with fear, somehow knowing it was true even though I had never suspected it.

"You killed her," I whispered, covering my trembling mouth with my hand and shaking my head. "You killed Elyse."

Nick grunted, "They all should have died when that boat went down. Unfortunately the plug didn't let go as soon as I planned. Elyse was the only one who was too weak to make it to shore."

I felt my knees start to knock and I willed myself to remain calm. I put my hand down and moved it further along the stove handle, feeling the roughened fabric of the towel as I stared at the arrogant monster before me.

"In the end, it was for the best," his chuckle grated on my nerves. "If Declan had died then, I never would have been able to accomplish everything else I've pulled off."

He faced Mr. Talcos, his grip tightening on the gun, "And your death would have cheated me of seeing you stripped from all you love in life."

The gun bobbed in his right hand. "First your wife, then your children, then your grandchildren, your company and finally your reputation. Everything you worked for in life, gone."

He snapped the fingers of his left hand and I gasped. The depth of his depravity overwhelmed me. Unfortunately, my compulsory sound drew his attention back to me.

"It's a shame you became involved, Aimee." The way he said my name filled me with dread and I wanted to lash out, but I held my tongue. "If you had only been able to resist Declan, but, unfortunately for you, you were immediately smitten."

I didn't bother to deny what he said. I might not have felt for Declan what I was learning to feel for Adam, but our bond had been real. Trying to divert Nick from my relationship, I asked him what I still didn't know.

"If Declan knew it was you, why was he protecting his grandfather?"

Nick laughed arrogantly. "He didn't know it was me. The day before he left, we met and I convinced him his grandfather was behind the heist. I had papers, accounts and numbers to back me up. He not only believed me, he was willing to take the rap for him."

The pieces fell into place. Declan and I coming to the Maine house before Declan thought his grandfather would be there. Declan searching his grandfather's computer. Making plans to leave the country as soon as he knew for sure where the money had gone. He might have told Howard Angle that his grandfather was set up in order to protect him but in his heart he knew he had to accept the possibility of his guilt and then set out to know, one way or the other.

Declan's desire to have me as a go between was because he couldn't trust his grandfather. I also realized that somewhere in the back of his mind, Declan didn't believe the evidence, even as Nick spelled it out to him. He was wrestling with what he saw with his eyes and what he knew in his heart.

My heart ached for the man I had married but never really known; for the doubts he had suffered, for the burden he had carried. At this moment I knew I would never regret saying yes to Declan the night he asked me for help in that stupid stadium bathroom.

I looked at the evil man sitting before me. I needed to wipe some of the smugness from his face.

"Declan knew the truth in the end?" I asked tightly.

"Of course," Nick bragged. "I told him, right before he died."

"So you didn't really win, then," I said, feeling a surge of triumph. "He knew his grandfather wasn't a thief."

Nick's lips pressed together in a thin line as my statement penetrated his consciousness. Then he shook his head violently, as if casting out the idea.

"No!" he shouted, rising from the stool and pointing his gun at me. "He knew I had won because he knew that after he was dead, only his grandfather was left to take the blame. And," his voice ended triumphantly, "he knew I had killed Elyse."

His gaze shifted to Mr. Talcos. "He also knew I was going to make it out of the country with enough money to live a life of luxury, after I destroyed his company."

His last words meant nothing to me. Did he mean by stealing the money, the company would have to fold? I looked at Mr. Talcos whose shoulders slumped. He was barely listening.

Nick's eyes were blazing as I turned back towards him and I involuntarily caught my breath at the hatred I saw burning there. Slowly I inched closer to the towel, not really having a plan but throwing out a question to keep him talking.

"Why didn't you leave the country right away? Right after you killed Declan? It would have been so much easier."

*And I wouldn't be in this situation right now*, I thought.

My question appeared to please him. I think he liked explaining just how great his plan had been.

"For two reasons really." Nick's gun arm relaxed at his side though he continued to point it at me. "First, I didn't want to appear suspicious during the FBI's investigation. Second, I wasn't done yet."

The candle lowered and I could barely see his face, but then the flame grew again, reflecting on his teeth. He was smiling.

Suddenly he whirled the gun towards my grandfather-in-law who sat hunched, barely holding himself up on the stool.

"You have no idea what I've been doing, do you?"

Mr. Talcos' lifted his head slightly in response.

"All your precious research that led to the discovery of the Zika vaccine is being published by your competition. The shot itself will soon be released on the market, and not by Autem Viris."

Mr. Talcos' ragged voice spoke up, "You sold our research findings?"

Nick laughed vindictively. "You're losing everything, Alfred, everything."

"Why did you kill Declan?" Mr. Talcos' question came across weakly, almost lost in the shadow.

"He knew too much. He would have stopped me from completing what I had started. And he belonged to you."

I shivered, the hatred couching his statement making me nauseas.

"How did you know where to find him?"

"I waited until he contacted me. That was the easy part."

"But you had an alibi," I interjected, remembering what Adam had told me. "Why did your secretary say she saw you the morning of Declan's murder?"

"Everyone has their price," he answered, not changing the position of the gun but I saw his silhouette in the near dark shift towards me.

"Why did you threaten me? And ransack my room?"

Nick became supercilious. "That was a slight miscalculation on my part. Declan told me before I killed him that he had known all along I'd been stealing from the company. He led me to believe he had proof and he wasn't afraid to use it. I thought maybe you had it. I'm afraid I believed him for a time but I soon realized it was just a ploy to stop me from shooting him."

That also explained why he had broken into Mr. Talcos' safe.

My heart throbbed in the silence that followed and in a small voice I asked the most important question, "What are you going to do to us?"

Even as I asked, I didn't want to know.

"Mr. Talcos is going to sign a letter saying he not only embezzled the money but he sold the bioresearch secrets to his competitor, essentially destroying his own company."

Before he had a chance to continue, Mr. Talcos interrupted, "That's how you'll ruin my reputation?" His voice broke and I knew he was defeated. "As the ultimate revenge?"

Nick laughed pretentiously. "That's how this is going to play out, old man."

Slowly I eased the towel from the oven towards me, not taking my eyes from the barely visible man in front of me. At this point I had no idea where his gun was directed but I knew time was running out.

"Your competitor is ready to release their discovery of the Zika vaccine to the media this week. Unfortunately for you, you will already have been found dead with a self-inflicted wound after killing your newly acquired, and shall I add lovely, granddaughter-in-law. To make it just a little more pathetic, you will be clutching your wife's ring and your children's hair. Tragic, really."

As he laughed, the light from the candle flared and I could see his face. The gleam was fiendish and I racked my brain for anything to stall him.

Grasping at straws, I threw out, "How did you do it? How did you steal the money? And the research?"

Nick's conceited countenance turned my stomach. "I've been working with that company for over fourteen years. They seldom notice where I go or what I do. It was easy to slip into the lab and copy notes and other information off their computers."

He literally spit out the words, "The embezzlement? That was even easier. Everyone and their mother knew that Declan kept the USB with all his personal account information in his safe. I just staged a diversion one day when I was in his office and the safe was open. It took less than three minutes to copy it."

The flame from the candle grew and threw light around the kitchen. Trembling, I watched as Nick's gaze passed over my face. My repulsed expression must have given me away because a mask slid down and he pushed away from the counter.

His sudden movement caused the stool he had been sitting on earlier to fall over with a loud clatter. In the instant he was distracted by the noise, I grabbed the towel and flung it as quickly as possible towards the flickering candle. I watched as in the blink of an eye it caught the glass holder and knocked it to the ground, shattering and at the same moment cloaking us in darkness.

Nick hurled curses at me as I crouched down and ran as quickly as a blind person away from the kitchen. I flinched, waiting to hear gunshots, and hoping Mr. Talcos had known enough to duck down.

I pictured the hallway from the kitchen to the foyer and tried to figure out where to go. My initial impulse was to run away as fast as I could from the house, but I also knew that I probably wouldn't get very far. Nick was nothing if not bigger and faster than I and, if we were going to make it, I needed to get help immediately.

Opening and then slamming the front door in an effort to divert Nick, I quickly dived into the hall closet that adjoined the entryway, trying to silence my breathing as I stood with the door open a crack. I watched as Nick ran by, his way illuminated by a phone flashlight, and then he opened the front door. I bit my lip and tried to mentally will him to leave the house. He stood there a moment before going completely outside. The breath I released should have been loud enough to hail him back inside.

In the second it took him to walk to the edge of the porch, I stepped out of the closet and quietly shut the door, resisting the urge to slam it. I quickly locked the deadbolt before heading upstairs.

The sound of Nick's persistent banging started almost immediately and I tried to drown it out as I half-ran, half-crawled up the stairs. I heard gulping sobs and realized they were mine. As I made it to the entrance of my room it penetrated my consciousness that the rain had stopped and a thin sliver of moonlight was now making its way through the window.

Its glow illuminated the chair enough that I could make out my purse dumped sideways and more than half the contents spilled on the floor. Realizing I had inadvertently spilled it while searching in the dark earlier, I ran over and began feeling around on the floor for my phone.

What felt like minutes went by and I sensed myself panicking. Below I could still hear pounding intermixed with the faint curses of a very angry man. I fleetingly thought of Mr. Talcos in the kitchen but even if he needed my help, there was nothing I could do for him.

At the moment my hand came into contact with the hard plastic case covering my phone, a gunshot went off and I knew that Nick had found a way to enter the house. Grabbing my cell back from beneath the drapery where it had fallen, I hurriedly turned it over and lifted the cover.

My hands shook as I pushed the *on* button. I tried to hold my finger steady enough to touch the emergency icon but it shook so much I was on my fourth try before I heard ringing on the line.

Someone answered just as I thought to close the bedroom door. Turning, I saw the gleaming eyes and maniacal countenance of Nick Santos standing in the entryway.

# Chapter 27

"Very clever," he said, advancing into the room. I could see the gun in his hand and it didn't waver for a second as he slowly came towards me.

I panicked; it's the only excuse for what I did. Screaming into the phone that someone was trying to murder me, I threw it at his face and then tried to pull the curtain down.

I don't know what I was thinking. Actually, I think in that moment I was just reacting. I had nowhere to go and I didn't want to die.

The phone hit Nick squarely in the nose but he didn't seem to notice. The sound of the woman on the other end of the line continued, asking questions, and simultaneously telling me to remain calm.

I held the torn curtain up between us and looked into his eyes as he proceeded with deliberate steps until he stood less than a foot away.

"Aimee," he said, his voice wafting through the air and effectively drowning out the emergency operator's continued insistence that someone talk to her. "I have an idea."

He took a step closer and I defensively took a step back, running into the windowsill.

He slowly cocked the gun away from me and I watched him warily, unsure what he would do next.

"Why don't you come with me? You did it once for Declan, didn't you? Made a split second decision to go with someone you didn't know, on a whim?"

His voice became creepily persuasive, "I would take good care of you."

His offer scared me even more than his threat of killing me. In the back of my mind I realized he was once again trying to possess what he perceived belonged to the Talcos family, but I also was confident that he would destroy whatever he couldn't have.

With the moonlight streaming through the completely uncovered glass, I could make out his features. Without saying a word, I shook my head in defiance, not taking my eyes from his.

He took another step towards me and I pressed myself as close to the window as I possibly could. There really wasn't any more room.

His voice lowered and his eyes softened. A terror I had never known began to inch over me. "You have nothing left. Come with me."

Still I shook my head. The phone had gone silent and I wondered briefly if the woman on the other end had taken me seriously. Even if she had, no one would get there in time.

In one last desperate attempt, I screamed, "Never!" and rushed him.

I threw the curtain over the gun and began yanking down with all my weight. I was lucky that he had already tilted the pistol away from me, because when it went off, it went wide and shattered the window instead of my head.

I became a crazy woman, holding onto the curtain still wrapped around his arm as I tried to stand and dodge away, effectively causing him to spin and fall. This should have freed me to run, but I wasn't strong enough. Even as I leapt past him, he grabbed onto the back of my shirt with his free hand and dragged me, fighting the entire way, towards him.

I looked up in time to see him rise above me, his gun hand still caught up in the curtain. His silhouette was outlined by the moonlight glowing behind him from the window and I knew he was about to strike me.

I flinched, closing my eyes, and waited for the impact.

It never came. Nick's weight was pushed away from me and I heard my shirt tear before his fierce grip slackened. An unknown assailant was now grappling for the gun and I knew without being able to see him clearly that it was Adam.

I scrambled away and then stood, looking for some instrument that would help. By the time I decided to try lifting the chair and hitting Nick over the back with it, Adam had subdued him with several well-placed punches to the jaw.

Then Adam sat back, breathing heavily, and said between gulps of air, "Are you okay?"

While I tried to think of a way to honestly answer him, the electricity popped back on. The bedside lamp filled the room with artificial light and the clock began to blink 12:00 in bright red numbers.

I looked over at Adam in relief and watched him climb off of Nick's chest, a hand bleeding and a look of concern on his face. I stumbled over, treading on unsteady legs, and tried to throw myself into his arms.

His smile welcomed me, but he held me back with his uninjured hand, nodding toward Nick. "I want nothing more than to hold you right now, darling. But we need to get this guy into custody."

I looked down at the unconscious form lying at our feet and shivered. How one man could be so evil and hurt so many people was unfathomable to me and yet here he was.

I wanted to help Adam tie up Nick as we waited for backup, but I was trembling and breathing so hard that

Adam made me sit down on the edge of the bed and put my head between my knees before I passed out. Then he started trussing Nick up.

I sat in this rather unflattering position until my respirations slowed. As the tingling in my extremities cleared and the lightheadedness improved, I realized just how close to fainting I had been.

Still bent over, I listened as Adam reported in on his phone. Nick was just starting to moan as I straightened up, his wrists locked in handcuffs behind him and one foot chained to the leg of the bed.

"How did you know to come?" I asked when Adam was done, no doubt a bit of hero worship in my tone.

Adam looked up from his phone. "I was coming over, remember?"

I nodded but that seemed so long ago now. I felt my breathing accelerate and put my head back between my knees.

"Do you need to lie down?" Adam asked, coming rapidly to my side in two long strides and rubbing my shoulders. I sat back up. He tilted my chin with his uninjured hand and regarded me intently.

Shaking my head to clear it, I suddenly remembered Mr. Talcos. By the time I was able to lucidly communicate that the poor man was probably hurt and needed our help, the room had filled with police.

Adam immediately gave orders for someone to accompany him downstairs and turned to leave me. I reached out and grasped the wrist of his injured arm, noticing the blood was already dry on his knuckles. I called his name weakly.

He stopped and looked down where I still sat on the bed, his expression telling me to stay put.

"Please, Adam," I begged, strength I didn't know I possessed slowly coming to me, "I need to see him. I need to see if he's okay."

Adam's countenance fell and he glanced toward the officer who would be accompanying him before considering me again. "Darling, what if he's not? I think I'd better check and then I'll come back and tell you."

I stood, albeit a little wobbly, and insisted, "That's my grandfather down there. I need to go with you."

Adam stared at me a moment, probably calculating how strong I was to withstand another possible shock before taking my hand. Together we went downstairs to find Mr. Talcos.

We found him unconscious on the kitchen floor. His forehead sported a large gash and I worried that he could have more than a concussion. As Adam called for an ambulance, his buddy tried to staunch the bleeding with the kitchen towel I'd used not so long ago to put out the candle. I fleetingly hoped he'd shaken all the broken glass out of it.

I sat stroking Mr. Talcos' hand and crooning words of encouragement to him. He was breathing but he wasn't moving. Adam finished his call and then came and knelt beside me, his arm supporting my upper back.

It seemed to take forever for EMS to arrive. There were a lot of questions and I was encouraged to go to the hospital and get checked out more than once. I declined each time but told them I would be going to the emergency department shortly to be with Mr. Talcos. If something developed in the meantime, I would let a doctor examine me.

Throughout, Adam stayed by my side, not saying anything but gently keeping his arm around me. I saw Mr. Talcos loaded on the stretcher and rolled out to the waiting ambulance. Thankfully Nick Santos was removed from my bedroom without me witnessing that ordeal.

Finally things began to calm down. Police were still in the kitchen and my bedroom, collecting evidence, but Adam quietly led me away from the bustle and into the living room.

As we approached the sofa, I gave in to my weakness and sagged against him. Catching me, he carried me the rest of the way to the couch before sitting and cradling me in his lap. He stroked my hair and whispered soothing words while I cried into the crook of his neck.

Eventually my sobs turned to sniffling and I pulled back to see that I had soaked his shirt. Ineffectually patting it, I looked up and found him looking at me with a tender smile.

"How did you know to come upstairs?" I asked, thinking back to his rescue. "How did you know that I needed you?"

His smile turned into a grin and he leaned forward to press a kiss to my forehead.

"I didn't, not at first." He coughed slightly and then tried again, "I was stopping by to check on you. I almost didn't come because I'd texted you and you didn't answer. I thought you were probably asleep, but something wouldn't let me rest until I knew for certain that you were okay. As soon as I came up the front steps and saw the door was open with a bullet through the lock, well, I knew something was very, very wrong."

"You were just in time," I told him huskily, and then snuggled back into his chest.

After we sat quietly for a few more minutes, Adam asked me to tell him what had happened.

Slowly and hesitantly I told him what Nick had said, about the double murder, the embezzlement, the selling of research secrets, the childhood link and the hatred that he had harbored against the Talcos family for so many decades. I cried again as I told him how Nick had deliberately led Declan to believe his grandfather was a criminal and how he had killed him in cold blood after telling him about the murder of his sister.

Through it all Adam listened quietly, every once in a while agreeing with me when I would grow angry and say something about Nick, but mostly just noting what I said.

When I was done he hugged me tightly and murmured something about almost losing me. A delicious warmth spread through me, filling my heart with a comfortable sense of safety and belonging.

Feeling his lips press against my temple once again, I pulled back to face him. Our gazes locked and for a moment, time stopped moving.

"Aimee," he breathed, his eyes searching mine, a question hovering there.

I swallowed, suddenly unable to see or think about anything other than Adam Harrison.

"Yes?"

"I haven't asked you this before, because I didn't want to know. But now I need to. Did you love him?"

I was not expecting this. Adam had rarely alluded to Declan or my marriage after those first few days of the investigation. He had never seemed to care if we loved each other or if our marriage had been one merely for our mutual benefit.

"Does that matter?"

His gaze became uncertain and he lifted a hand to stroke a wayward lock behind my ear. "I don't know. I guess I'm trying to gauge how much time you need to heal."

He continued to caress my hair. "But that's not really possible, is it? Grief isn't something you can put a stop date on."

His hand stilled and slid to cup my face. I rested my cheek into his palm and then reached up and covered his hand with mine.

"I'm not broken," I said huskily, "I never was. I mourn his loss because I mourn the loss of a good man. I was confused at first and I might have at one point thought I was falling in love with Declan, but that was just because I'd never been in love before. I didn't know what love really is."

Adam's eyes darkened and he leaned closer, his breath warming my face. The vulnerability I saw in his expression touched something deep within me.

"And do you know what it is now?"

Like before, I was drawn to him as to a magnet.

"I think I'm learning."

Just as his lips lightly brushed mine, a chipper young voice interrupted, "Well, sir, we've got the house pretty much cleaned up."

A rookie stood there, his smile giving away that he knew exactly what he was doing when he interrupted us. Adam looked annoyed and I laughed as I slid from his lap and stood up.

Strangely enough, I felt like a load had been taken off me. Just talking about it with Adam had cleared my mind. Knowing I was safe now was probably also a key factor and knowing that Adam cared for me, well, that was definitely the clincher.

As the young officer talked with Adam, I slipped three of my fingers into his side pocket and waited.

The scout left and Adam looked apologetic as he held up his phone.

"I just have to make one phone call," he said.

"Do you think we could go check on Mr. Talcos afterwards?" I asked, pulling him towards me by his jeans, knowing visiting the elderly man was the right thing to do even though the regard in Adam's eyes was giving me other ideas.

His gaze dropped to my lips and I laughed at his obviously reluctant agreement. While he began to dial his phone, I slipped upstairs to get my shoes.

After putting them on, I looked around, taking in the damaged curtain rod hanging from the wall and the glass that still littered the floor. Searching among the broken shards, I checked for my phone but it must have been removed. I wondered if it was now considered evidence. Looking at the aftermath, it was hard to believe how much had happened in just one night.

I thought sadly of Nick, how he had let one event in his life not only ruin him but turn him into an instrument of destruction in the lives of so many others. As happens so often with the sin of pride, he had risen above his state in life only to fall lower than where he began.

Adam appeared in the doorway at that moment and disturbed my musings. I smiled at him as I walked from beside the bed where I'd put on my shoes to where he waited with outstretched fingers. Accepting my hand, he latched on firmly and we headed out the door together.

"Not scared?" he asked as we started down the stairs.

"Not a bit," I answered.

## THE END

## ABOUT THE AUTHOR

 Elizabeth was born and raised in New England where she happily worked for 12 years as a nurse in a community hospital. Things took a turn in 2015 when she found herself quitting her job, renting out her house and finding temporary care for her two dogs. She then embarked on a year-long mission to Guatemala where she worked in an orphanage, learned Spanish and began to take risks. In between cleaning scratched knees, hiking volcanoes, and learning to love frijoles, she discovered a new love in writing. Though her year in Central America has ended, Elizabeth returns home with the firm conviction that a new adventure is just beginning.

www.ingramcontent.com/pod-product-compliance
Lightning Source LLC
Chambersburg PA
CBHW050418260626
47156CB00003B/1056